TROPHY HUNTERS

A HALLEY BROWN MYSTERY

LEAH R CUTTER

KNOTTED ROAD PRESS

Trophy Hunters
A Halley Brown Mystery
Copyright © 2020 Leah Cutter
All rights reserved
Published by Knotted Road Press
www.KnottedRoadPress.com

ISBN: 978-1-64470-173-7

Cover Art:
ID 39755224 © Sergey Popov | Dreamstime.com
ID 178339778 © Anatolii Riabokon | Dreamstime.com

Cover and interior design copyright © 2020 Knotted Road Press
http://www.KnottedRoadPress.com

Reviews
It's true. Reviews help me sell more books. If you've enjoyed this story, please consider leaving a review of it on your favorite site.

Come someplace new…
Are you a traveler? Do you enjoy exploring strange new worlds, new cultures, new people?

Journey into the various lands envisioned by Leah Cutter.

Sign up for my newsletter and I'll start you on your travels with a free copy of my book, *The Island Sampler*. I will never spam you or use your email for nefarious purposes. You can also unsubscribe at any time.

http://www.LeahCutter.com/newsletter/

Forgotten Gods

A Wind Blown Torment

A Stone Strewn Clash

A Sea Washed Victory

Tanish Empire Trilogy

The Glass Magician

The Desert Heart

The Ghost Dog

The Shadow Wars Trilogy

The Raven and the Dancing Tiger

The Guardian Hound

War Among the Crocodiles

The Chronicles of Franklin

Franklin Versus The Popcorn Thief

Franklin Versus The Soul Thief

Franklin Versus The Child Thief

Huli Intergalactic - Science/Space Fantasy

Origins

The Strawberry Girl

Contemporary Fantasy

Siren's Call

The Immortals' War

Dalton slipped his trophy onto his wrist—this bitch's fitness watch. Dumbass cunt wasn't used to drinking. She was too *athletic* to do that sort of thing, didn't want to spoil that long lean body of hers.

However, she'd believed Dalton when he'd told her that the cocktail he'd ordered for her barely had any alcohol at all.

Silly cunt.

It had been easy to separate her from her so-called friends, to keep her drinking with him up at the bar. They must have thought she was a stuck-up bitch as well, given how easily they'd left her. They'd all come from their latest volleyball match, from the place up the street that had actual sand courts.

Only in yuppified Seattle, a neighborhood like Georgetown, would you find that sort of thing.

The bar in the front part of the distillery wasn't much. Square room, modern concrete floor, high ceiling "artistically" covered in industrial pipes, with a few tables and a plain counter at the back. Wooden shelves behind the bar held fat clear bottles with the bar's signature vodka.

Past the bar, down a narrow, dark hallway, hid the two

bathrooms. The hall ended at the actual distillery—closed for the night, though Dalton had tried the door to see how hard it would have been to break in there.

Would be a unique place for a nice bitch ride. But the door had not only been locked but armed, and he hadn't wanted to push his luck.

Dalton kept the latest bitch to his right, while Rick and Vern were chilling at a table to his left. They'd all gotten much better at the game: finding their newest ride, getting her to drink just a little too much, avoiding any cameras or interested bartenders when they slipped her the good stuff, then taking her into the bathroom or out back behind the bar and taking turns riding her.

They never took her to their car or back to their place. Too easy for even a drugged bimbo to identify them later. And they always wore condoms—couldn't take a chance on being identified that way, either. They all wore plain shirts and jeans, no logos or anything noticeable. They never arrived at a bar together. The three of them frequently pretended they didn't know each other.

They did take prizes. This was Dalton's third fitness watch. Vern clipped a small lock of hair. Rick hadn't settled on his thing yet, though he had kept the panties from the first chick, and just a sock from the second.

This bitch was just about loosened up enough. She had this wild red hair, like a mane, that she was shaking, trying to argue with Dalton.

"No, I wouldn't have left home without my watch!"

That southern accent of hers had almost been cute at first. Now, it was just a whine.

"But you did!" Dalton told her. She'd even told him her name at one point. Vickie? Valorie? Something with a V. "Don't you remember?"

She shook her head. Her eyes were glassy, though it was

kind of hard to see in the dim light of the bar. Then she tilted her head back, until it fell on the back of her neck.

"Would I leave without it?" she mused.

All this argument over a damned fitness watch. Stupid chick was just obsessed with it.

Fortunately, was too far gone to see it sitting, right there, on Dalton's wrist.

"Maybe you left it in the bathroom," Dalton suggested.

Her head toppled forward. He reached out a hand so she wouldn't fall off the barstool.

"Maybe I did!" she said.

"I'll help you go look," Dalton said, standing and sliding an arm around her.

She was skinny, just how he liked them. Lean and athletic, too.

Just right for breaking in.

"Okay, honey," she said, sliding closer to him. "My, you do smell fine."

Dalton shot a grin at the guys. Yeah, she was hot to trot.

And he was going to be the first to set her through her paces.

DALTON DIDN'T LIKE KISSING the bitches on the mouth. That wasn't for him. Besides, sometimes they tried to take over a kiss, maybe even stick their tongue down his throat.

He was the one in charge here. The one in control. Not them.

The bathroom was tiny, just a shitter and a sink, the mirror lined with stickers from obscure bands. He'd have to take the bitch standing up. That was okay. He'd done that once before.

He shoved her hard against the closed door and started

feeling her up. She was all muscle, skin, and bone. He pushed up her athletic bra and sucked at her nipples, making them pucker up.

He'd dig his teeth in later, when she was further along.

God, he was hard. And she had to be so wet and ready, writhing against the bathroom door. He kept his hands on her shoulders to hold her still while he attacked her nipples.

She wouldn't remember what had happened, but she was going to be so sore.

"Tha's my watch," she murmured.

Stupid bitch had finally figured out what was happening. Good. But she was too far gone to fight him.

"Naw, that's my watch," he assured her. He slipped the hand wearing the watch down to unbutton her jeans.

"No, tha's MY watch," she insisted. She wrapped her hand around his wrist and yanked his arm up.

Oh shit.

He looked up into eyes that were no longer glazed.

Fucking Vern must not have put enough of the roofies in.

"What the fuck?" she said harshly, looking around. She stood up, supporting her own weigh.

Dalton yanked his arm out of her grasp, then reached past her, pulling the door open, banging it into her back. He took off down the hallway and straight out the door of the bar, not looking at Vern and Rick. They'd get the message.

Pure adrenaline coursed through his veins. He was panting. And hard. A cool night breeze blew through the sweat in his hair. Damn it! They were just—

"Hey!" came a shout from behind him.

Dalton stopped and turned, surprised. Was it one of the guys?

Oh fuck. It was the chick.

"That's my watch!"

Of course, he'd get the crazy one.

He took off up the street, figuring that she was too drunk, too stoned, to follow him.

The footsteps pounding behind him proved him wrong.

Shit. She was in better shape than he was. His only hope was losing her down one of the tiny streets in this part of Georgetown.

Dalton applied speed and raced around a corner.

Fucking chick followed him. Fortunately, she wasn't catching up to him. Not yet. The drugs seemed to have slowed her down some.

Where the hell were the guys?

There wasn't much on this street. Barely wide enough for two cars. Dumpsters lined the one side, too big to do a movie superhero move and yank one out into her path. Weeds and a chain link fence on the other side, blocking access to an abandoned office building.

There wasn't any place he could hide or lose her down here. At least the block wasn't that long.

Crap. He was panting but he could keep going. The adrenaline was starting to fade and he'd be dragging soon.

He turned left at the end of the street. Fucking homeless people were on the sidewalk. He even jumped over a pair of legs, kicked a second set.

Maybe they'd slow her down.

He took a chance and glanced back.

Nope. She was still bearing down on him hard.

Goddamn it! Maybe he should drop the watch.

Except she probably wouldn't notice. Would keep after him.

Fuck.

He raced past a closed convenience store on the corner, with bars on all the windows and a gate over the door, before he turned up the next small street.

More warehouses. No yards. Nothing to cut through and maybe lose this redheaded Terminator imposter.

At least the cars all parked along the one side of the street weren't moving. No witnesses.

He heard a car from behind him. Fuck. He risked a quick glance over his shoulder.

That was Vern's car. They were coming up close to the chick.

Holy shit! They'd just run into her.

Everything slowed down. She flew through the air like she weighed nothing. She landed hard, splayed out at his feet, like she was praying to him or something.

She wasn't moving.

Good. Stupid bitch.

He jogged back to the car, sliding into the back seat. "Woo!" he shouted after he got in the car. He pounded the front seat, shouting, "Go! Go! Go! Go!"

Vern backed the car up, popping out of the side street and onto the main street.

"Slow down," Rick advised. "Gotta drive like we didn't do nothing wrong."

"Did you see that?" Dalton said. He pounded the front seat with his hand again. "Did you see that crazy chick!"

"Dude," Rick said. He turned in his seat, looking back at Dalton. "Thought she was going to kick your ass." He looked excited, grinning widely.

"Dude," was all Dalton said in reply. "Fancy driving there," he added, patting Vern on the shoulder.

"Yeah, I'll have to clean the grill later, make sure nothing stuck," Vern said. He was always like that. Practical.

"Ooooof," Dalton said, sitting back and taking a deep breath.

"Buckle your seatbelt," Vern reminded him.

"Yes, Mom," Dalton said. But he did as he was asked.

They didn't want to give the cops any reason to pull them over. Particularly not for something as stupid as not wearing a seatbelt.

The adrenaline started to fade. Tomorrow, his legs and feet might be a little sore from running.

He was still hard, too. Hadn't been able to get his ride. Though it had been kind of cool, running away from her. He looked at his newest prize. It was black and sleek. Unisex, so it didn't look out of place on his own wrist.

He knew he was going to have to turn off the GPS so the stupid watch couldn't track him. But he could do that later.

He squirmed on the seat and adjusted himself. Yeah, he was going to jack off as soon as he got home, remembering the one who got away.

Next time, they'd be smarter about it. Their ride wasn't going to come up too soon for them to have their fun.

The next day, hearing about the hit-and-run death in Georgetown just made Dalton hard all over again.

CHAPTER 2

"WHICH MEANS THAT MY SISTER, Victoria, has been murdered!" Halley's newest client, Amber Lee, exclaimed dramatically. "It wasn't simply a hit and run."

Halley tried hard not to roll her eyes. Technically, Amber Lee wasn't a client yet. Halley frequently gave people a free thirty-minute consultation while she decided whether or not she'd accept their case as a private investigator. Or their shit.

"What exactly is this thing that's missing?" Halley asked, delaying the inevitable stormy scene when she turned Amber Lee down and told her to go somewhere else with her wild theories about an accident that had occurred six months ago. Halley took another sip of her excellent coffee, glad that they were meeting in the small conference room at her shared office space and not out in public somewhere, as she doubted that would level out Amber Lee's histrionics.

The late afternoon sun highlighted the trees outside the windows of the old converted mansion. After all the rain that spring, Halley was itching to get this last meeting of the day over with so she could be outside while it was still clear. Hell, she could even see blue skies out there.

Reluctantly, Halley dragged her attention back from the

tempting sunshine to the woman sitting at the head of the conference table, her back to the lovely window. The meeting room was a nice mix of professional and homey, with a sleek blond-wood oval conference table; black, ergonomic office chairs; and beautifully refinished built-in cupboards on the side wall, with the original leaded glass doors, holding the coffee and tea supplies, as well as spare pens, notepads, and a rainbow of colored Post-it notes.

If describing Amber Lee for a police report, Halley would say that the woman in front of her was a Caucasian female between the ages of forty and fifty, five-foot-three, one hundred and seventy pounds. Strawberry blonde hair that was natural as well as thinning, with fine wisps that curled around her round face and hazel eyes. She was dressed as an office worker in a dark green cotton blouse with a fussy collar, black slacks, and cheap shoes with extra support.

"Victoria was obsessed with fitness," Amber Lee explained. Her voice held a twang to it—Texas, Halley would guess. "She'd go on and on about all her workouts, how much weight she was pressing, how many miles she ran, how often she got to the gym."

Halley easily read between the lines—Victoria's talk about her workouts was a passive-aggressive way of needling her sister about her weight. Halley's own older sister Caroline excelled at that sort of thing, though her comments were generally about how much work Caroline had to do taking sole care of their mother, back in Spokane.

"So Victoria always had this fitness watch, you know, one of those devices for measuring her heart rate, timing her runs, keeping track of all that busy work she was doing," Amber Lee said. "She would never have gone out of the house without it. Period."

"But the police didn't find it on her body," Halley said slowly. That did seem strange. One of the cops she used to work with had been just as obsessed. He'd even bought a waterproof one so he could wear it in the shower and never had to take it off.

Halley had understood that he'd been hazing her, emphasizing that he'd been wearing the watch while naked. However, it had been so junior varsity compared to the other shit she'd received that she'd barely noted it at the time.

"That's right! The police did not find it on Victoria! They returned all her other belongings to me. Including Mama's ring, that Victoria inherited when Mama died two years ago," Amber Lee said with extra emphasis.

"Could the device have been thrown from her body due to the crash?" Halley asked.

"No, ma'am, it couldn't," Amber Lee said. "It was too hardy. An ugly black thing. She couldn't have just flung it away."

"When exactly did this hit and run occur?" Halley asked.

"November eighteenth, last year," Amber Lee said, her eyes starting to glisten with tears again. "Just coming up on six months."

Halley nodded. She didn't remember reading anything about the accident. Then again, it had happened in Georgetown, a rundown neighborhood south of Seattle that was slowly being gentrified.

"What did the detective in charge say when you asked him about it?" Halley said. Damn it! She didn't want to take this case. Amber Lee was going to be a handful and a half to deal with. Plus, surely whoever had caught the case was doing their job.

Halley had worked in the Seattle police department for three years before leaving when it became clear that her dyslexia was going to hold her back from ever getting her detective's shield. It was impossible for her to write the types of reports that the brass wanted. So instead, she'd quit and started her own detective agency six years ago.

She really, *really* didn't want to have to contact the precinct about one of her cases. It always felt like rubbing salt in an old wound that would never heal.

"He didn't even bother to write down the information," Amber Lee said, pointedly looking at the blank space in front of Halley on the conference table.

"Who is the detective in charge?" Halley asked, deliberately sitting back further in her chair and taking another sip of her coffee. She hated taking notes in front of a client. They might see her bad spelling and the way she reversed letters and words. If she really had to take notes, she would set up a recorder, then pay for a transcription service. That way, her notes would be in order if they were subpoenaed. That had happened twice since she'd started her agency, during cases where Halley had had to be in touch with the SPD.

Fortunately, Halley had been blessed with a good memory for faces and facts. Working as a police officer, then as a detective, had really honed that skill.

"Detective Branson," Amber Lee said. "Now mind you, that man was polite enough. But he didn't take me seriously when I brought him the new evidence."

That didn't surprise Halley. She knew Detective Branson. He was a quiet man, his blond hair thinning and turning silver over the years. His suits were on the cheaper side, and in some shade of brown. He'd always struck her as thorough though, making sure that every piece of paperwork was filled in and filed appropriately. However, Amber Lee would rub every single one of his nerves the wrong way.

"Why do you think it was murder and not a hit and run?" Halley said.

Amber dramatically pulled out a sheaf of papers, slapping them down on the table.

"Look at that heartrate reading!" Amber Lee said, shoving one of the graphs in front of Halley. "It's all over the place."

Halley nodded, looking at the blurry graph. The line across the bottom started low, then jumped up to a higher setting, then took a third jump before finally tapering off and then abruptly ending.

"See that dashed line near the start?" Amber Lee said, pointing with a finger that needed a new manicure at least a week ago. "That shows when she took the tracker off. Or when someone took it off her. When it wasn't registering her heartbeat."

"So she, or someone, took the watch off here, then someone else put it on here?" Halley asked. "So this part of the graph is someone else's heartbeat?" The heartbeat before the dashed line was significantly lower than after the dashed line.

"Exactly!" Amber Lee said, like a proud Mama. "Then, here," she said, pointing at the next jump in the heartrate, "that's when she realized it was missing. The guy who stole it would take off running, with Victoria chasing after him."

"If she was chasing him, then who hit her?" Halley said. Damn it! She didn't want to have to try to subpoena the records for this case or something. Not that she could. As it was considered vehicular homicide, it was still an open case.

"His buddies," Amber Lee said sagely, as if it were obvious.

Halley shook her head and sat back again. "There isn't much to go on," she said slowly. Even if Victoria was chasing after whoever had stolen her watch, that didn't mean "his buddies" had deliberately struck Victoria with their car.

"Because it was a hit and run, vehicular homicide, they

did a toxicology report," Amber Lee said. "She had Rohypnol in her system."

That didn't make sense to Halley. "How could she have been chasing after someone if she'd been given a roofie?"

"She was a red-head, like me," Amber Lee said, reaching up a pudgy hand to pat at her own thinning hair. "She needed more Novocain anytime she had her teeth worked on, and she'd go through it faster than a normal person. Whoever drugged her didn't give her enough."

Halley vaguely remembered reading something about that, how red-heads did need more anesthesia than a regular patient.

"Plus, there's been two additional reports, one in Georgetown and one in Sodo, of women swearing that they'd been roofied and gang raped," Amber Lee said, adding to the papers that were already on the conference table between them.

That was bad, Halley had to admit. Because for every woman who reported assault, there had to be dozens of cases, if not over a hundred, that had occurred when the woman hadn't stepped forward.

"Where did Victoria's hit and run occur?" Halley said, trying to get a better picture.

"As I said, in Georgetown. In one of those horrid neighborhoods that's just warehouses," Amber Lee said. "I've only gone there once. It was awful. But I told Victoria that she shouldn't go gallivanting all about town like she did, running everywhere."

"Do you think that's why she was there? Because she'd gone for a run?" Halley asked. "Where did she live?"

"Up in Magnolia, of course," Amber Lee said. She sniffed suddenly, her eyes growing watery. "Where else would two southern belles end up?"

Halley could tell that had been a common refrain between the two sisters.

However, going down to Georgetown for a run after ten o'clock at night, during the middle of the week, seemed rather strange.

"And nothing else was missing," Halley said. "Her wallet was with her?"

Amber Lee nodded. "And her keys, and her bus pass."

"Did she take the bus down to Georgetown for her run?" Halley asked. That didn't make much sense to her. "Or did she run all the way there?"

The triumphant smile that Amber Lee gave Halley filled her with unease.

"She went down there to play volleyball with that team of hers," Amber Lee said. "They'd all gone out to a bar afterwards. Then, they'd left her behind. She was found two blocks away, in the middle of a street. She wouldn't have gone for a run after a practice."

"I don't know," Halley said, sitting back again. "It's just a lot of conjecture."

"I think you should take the case," came a beautiful rich baritone voice from the doorway.

Halley turned to yell at whoever had opened the door. However, Phoenix stood there, paused and poised, looking as if they were ready for a glamour photograph.

Phoenix wore a beautiful pale blue gown, the color of rain-washed spring skies, showing off their huge fake breasts and feminine curves. It rose up to their neck, as Phoenix rarely showed off too much skin. One of their smaller tiaras sparkled in their dark, luxurious hair. White satin gloves that went to their elbows covered their hands, as usual. Today, Phoenix had on a neon-pink fur stole over their broad shoulders. Their makeup was flawless, and their dark beard was well trimmed.

"Hello, my dear," Phoenix said, gliding into the room.

Amber Lee's mouth was still open as she looked up.

"I'm so sorry for your loss," Phoenix continued in that incredibly smooth voice of theirs. They'd trained as an opera singer for many years and though they no longer performed, they did coach other singers.

"Why, thank you," Amber Lee said, finally coming back to herself. "I don't believe we've been properly introduced," she said, rising with a glare thrown at Halley.

"Phoenix, this is Amber Lee Wilson," Halley said, trying to suppress a grin. Finally, something that appeared to shut Amber Lee up. "Amber Lee, this is Phoenix."

"Miss Phoenix?" Amber Lee said. She seemed to realize that Phoenix wasn't about to shake hands with her—Phoenix didn't touch anyone readily, at least as far as Halley knew.

"Just Phoenix, my dear," they said. "Can you get us some tea?" Phoenix asked Halley without looking at her. "Now, tell me all about it."

Halley sighed but did as she'd been asked, in part because she really didn't want to have to hear any more of Amber Lee's histronics.

Phoenix had first come into Halley's life the previous winter and seemed determined to stay and be Halley's occasional sidekick, though generally when Phoenix was around, they were the star of the show. Any show.

Halley walked into the large kitchen of the converted mansion. It was empty—the other people who shared the co-working space were probably upstairs in their offices finishing off the last of their work for the day. The kitchen was large and modern, the newest room in the entire building. A massive gourmet stove took up a good chunk of the far wall. The farmhouse style concrete sink took up an equally large share on an adjoining wall.

Halley filled the electric kettle with water and set it to

heating while she got out a teapot and cups, placing them on a tray. Then she figured what the hell, and also arranged a few sugar cookies on a plate as well. She made herself another cup of coffee while the peppermint tea steeped. Once it was finished, she made her way back to the conference room.

"You'll be in good hands with Halley," Phoenix was promising Amber Lee as she came walking back in.

Swell. While Halley hadn't been completely certain that she wanted to take on Amber Lee, it appeared she had a new client after all.

CHAPTER 3

"Why do you want me to take Amber Lee as a client?" Halley had to ask once she'd finally gotten the woman out of the office.

"Poor dear is lonely," Phoenix said with an expressive wave of their bejeweled hand, the large (probably fake) diamonds glittering on all four gloved fingers.

"And?" Halley said, not allowing herself to be distracted.

"I would have thought a serial rapist would be right up your alley," Phoenix said. They cocked one eyebrow at Halley while they took another sip of their peppermint tea.

Halley shook her head. Though she did do criminal investigation as a private investigator, she still rarely dealt with those sorts of crimes. "Nope. Still don't believe you. What else is going on?" She sipped at her coffee, still warm in its special cup that kept it at the perfect temperature.

The cup had been a very thoughtful present this past Christmas from Phoenix, who couldn't help but notice Halley's coffee habit/obsession. (She lived in Seattle and had to fit in. Or at least that was how she justified it to herself.)

That the cup was also royal purple with a unicorn on the

side that said, "Keep life weird" didn't detract from the fact that Halley still loved it.

Phoenix gave a dramatic sigh. "Well, since you insist," they said, putting their cup down on the table between them. "It hasn't just been ciswomen who have been targeted," they said.

Bingo.

Figured. Phoenix tended to only get involved in cases that had a queer angle to them.

"Angel DeMure says that she was approached by a straight boy one night, when she'd been drinking down in Sodo. While he tried to get her drunk—having no idea of the fortitude of decadence he was approaching—one of his buddies came up on the side and put something in her drink." Phoenix sniffed in a disapproving manner. "Angel caught him at it. Ran the three of them off."

"Serial gang rapists?" Halley said, shuddering. That wasn't good. And it would be difficult to track, particularly if they took turns approaching women. There wouldn't be a single pattern to identify, but at least three.

Phoenix nodded grimly. "Amber Lee's story sounded enough like Angel's that I thought there might be something there."

Halley sighed. The case was cold. It had been six months since the vehicular homicide. There wouldn't be any clues at the scene of the crime, but Halley was still going to have to go see it. Amber Lee had managed to get most of the police reports and had turned them over to Halley. She'd spend the next day going over those.

Since it was an unsolved homicide, it was technically still considered an open case, though Halley knew that no one at the precinct was likely working on it anymore. She wasn't looking forward to contacting Detective Branson, and was going to try to avoid it at all costs.

At least Amber Lee hadn't been stingy about paying Halley's fees. She'd inherited her sister's estate. All the money from Victoria's life insurance policy, as well as her 401K, was going toward Halley solving the case.

Amber Lee had believed that her sister's death had been an accident to start with. It had taken her time to realize that something was wrong, that her sister's fitness watch wasn't with the body. Then, it had taken more time to get the passwords and access to her sister's fitness account.

Only after figuring out that the watch had continued to ping local towers long after Victoria's death had Amber Lee slowly come to the conclusion that someone had stolen Victoria's watch.

Halley still didn't see the leap though, from stolen watch to being killed.

"You know that Amber Lee is going to be a thorn in my side from here on out, right?" Halley said. She hadn't wanted to take the case because of Amber Lee. If she'd been a more reasonable person, maybe Halley would have been more open-minded about it.

It wasn't that assholes didn't need justice done. Just that someone else could do it.

"That's why I agreed to work with you, so that I could take her calls," Phoenix assured Halley.

"Okay," Halley said slowly. She hadn't been there for that part of the conversation, or at least didn't remember it.

"So what's our first step?" Phoenix asked brightly.

Halley looked outside. The lovely spring afternoon was long gone. "I'm going to go home and eat dinner," she announced. "Then spend the night watching TV and reading. Tomorrow is soon enough to start looking into this."

If she'd been hoping that Phoenix would be disappointed, well, that wasn't going to happen. Instead, Phoenix gave her a huge grin. "I was hoping you'd say that! I also have plans for the evening. But I was ready and willing to help. I can still cancel if you think I should, if there's something for us to do tonight."

"Fine," Halley said, trying but failing to not sound sour. She shook her head. Phoenix wasn't as bad as some of the drag queens that Halley had been working with recently, but they also weren't undramatic, not by any stretch of the imagination.

They said their goodbyes and Halley grabbed her coat before heading back to her tiny condo, just a few blocks away. The office was on Fifteenth, while her building was down on Twelfth. While she had an SUV that she loved, she generally kept it parked behind the condo building, walking or taking the bus everywhere and only using it when she needed to get someplace out of the way.

She'd have to check in the morning whether she would drive to Georgetown or take a bus. It might not be too bad to go ahead and drive there, and it would give her a chance to explore more of the neighborhood.

Halley lived on the top floor of a three-story brick building that had been built back in 1910, when a lot of the apartments in the area had been constructed. Her condo was barely four hundred square feet. There was one large living area/bedroom, a good sized bathroom, a closet that was almost as big, and a tiny kitchen. She mainly reheated food and didn't do much actual cooking.

As it was just down the hill from the shared office space, that meant Halley had even less occasion to drive.

People she passed were hurrying home from their jobs, or walking their stupid dogs. Halley found it irritating having to walk around them.

Fortunately, she had leftovers she could heat up, so she didn't have to go out and be with anyone that evening. She knew that as her mood grew more foul, she was more and more likely to tear the hide off someone.

Or get into a fight, just to take some fratboy down. There was a reason she trained in Krav Maga.

Her building was half a block off Thomas, one of the busier streets. Broad marble steps led up to the front door, which looked like the original, with the name of the building (The Hartley) done in gold leaf across the glass. A large brass plate had been installed at a later date, updating the lock. However, Halley knew that the front door wasn't really secure. No one on the board was willing to pay for the updates to get a good lock.

The front step of her building had a couple of packages waiting on it. She picked them up, fumbling for her keys.

Of course, opening the door was like walking into a fucking sauna, given how her day had been going. The building still had the original turn-of-the-last-century radiator system for heating. Though there had been talk of moving the thermostat out of the front hall, away from the door, no one had wanted to pay for that either. So the people in the building alternately sweated and froze during the winter months, depending on how long people left the front door open.

The furnace would be turned off on June first, regardless of how warm or cold it was. Which potentially meant more days freezing if they had yet another "Junuary" that year.

Other packages were piled onto the table right underneath the thermostat. Halley added the ones she'd picked up to the heap, glancing to see if there was anything for her. There shouldn't be: She used the office address most of the time because it was actually secure. Her sister Caroline was still an asshole, though, and might send something to her building anyway.

Not finding any packages addressed to her, Halley turned

and walked up the broad, once elegant staircase to her floor. The railing was carved out of a smooth wood that had been repainted a dark red recently. Halley hated touching it because it was always sticky. On the wall of the staircase, wooden wainscoting had been painted the same color. Above that, wallpaper ran to the top of the high ceiling. It had been replaced in the 1950s. It had a pale background, with gold stripes and roses running down the panels.

Like the rest of the building, the wallpaper had seen better days. Now, dark lines ran the width of it, fingers dragged along as residents climbed the stairs.

Halley locked and bolted the door behind her once she reached her place. It would take a serious battering ram to break into her condo. She felt a little safer here, though she was far too aware that there wasn't really anyplace safe, not for a woman on her own.

She'd carried Amber Lee's papers home with her, in her backpack. It would be difficult for anyone to steal them from Halley. The backpack was a traveler's bag, made from a knife-resistant material that had metal woven into it. The straps were damned near indestructible as well.

She kept the lights in her place off. There wasn't that much to walk into. To the left of the door was the original Murphy bed that had been built into the room. The front of it had a false white mantel. The mattress and the mechanism that kept it in place were new, and it made a good use of the small space.

In the opposite corner of the room Halley had her desk, along with a combination safe where she kept all her client paperwork. The safe itself would survive a fire. She'd needed to get it for insurance purposes. She put Amber Lee's papers in there, then hung her jacket up in her closet.

She kept her Glock in a gun safe that was bolted to the floor of her closet. It had been one of the biggest changes to her routine once she'd left the police force, to leave her gun behind. She was licensed to carry it—even had an armed private investigator license.

Police training would say, "Better safe than sorry" when it came to always carrying.

Halley had come to realize that she didn't want to rely on the false confidence a gun gave her, like relying on the badge.

She'd stepped out from behind that shield. Could no longer afford to be such an asshole to people, but had to be polite.

Times like this, though, the dark times, made it much more difficult to be kind.

Halley went into the tiny kitchen to reheat some leftovers. She still had noodles from her favorite place up on Broadway. Part of their gimmick was a noodle machine out front, where you could watch the noodles being made as you walked by. Fortunately, the food they made was tasty, andthere was always a lot of it.

The smell of garlic and ginger had her mouth already watering as she spooned the dish out into a bowl. Maybe she was just hungry.

She knew better. Tonight was likely to be a bad night.

Halley never kept any alcohol in her condo. Her mom was an alcoholic. Her sister was addicted to whatever she could lay her hands on, though in the past few months she had seemed to be cutting back.

Her dad—her bio-dad—hadn't had any issues that way, at least as far as Halley knew. She didn't know a lot about her bio-dad, having just found out earlier that year that the father who'd raised her hadn't actually donated any of his DNA.

Neither Halley nor Billy could figure out why their bio-dad had dallied with her mom. She'd tried checking with her mom's doctor, but he'd retired. She didn't remember her father being away on any business trips. He'd been a mechanic.

So how had her mom met Billy's dad?

Billy had a ton of old case notes that he'd grudgingly handed over to her. It had taken a couple of months to get through all of them.

A lot of hinky stuff had been going on that made Halley agree that there was a good possibility that their bio-dad hadn't committed suicide. But neither of them had managed to develop many more clues.

Halley had just sat down at her desk with her dinner and was about to turn on the TV to lose herself in some mindless show when her phone rang.

Lovely. Caroline. Her sister.

They'd fought and made up a bunch of times over the past few years. Caroline wasn't losing it, not yet. She'd also made an effort to clean up her act some. But Halley feared that her sister was circling the same drain their mother already rotated around.

However, neither Caroline nor their mom was willing to actually seek help. Or even to get out of the hell-hole of Spokane and come to the bright lights of the city.

"Hey," Halley said as she answered the phone, pushing her food to the side.

"Mom's in the hospital," Caroline said dramatically.

If this had been the first time, or possibly the second, Halley might have felt some fear.

This was one of an uncountable series of times. All she felt was dread.

"And?" Halley said when her sister didn't continue.

"She has pneumonia," Caroline finally added.

That was new. The last few times her mother had been hospitalized had been for falling and breaking something.

Again. It wasn't that her mother was clumsy. She was a drunk.

"What are her chances of actually getting out sober?" Halley had to ask.

"It won't matter if she does," Caroline said. "She'll just go right back on the booze."

"It doesn't help that you let her keep a stash around," Halley added, though she knew she shouldn't.

It was just a bad night. Might as well take it out on her sister as anyone else.

"Of course, you would say that. You think it's my fault that Mom's a drunk," Caroline snarled.

Halley knew it wasn't actually Caroline's fault. But her sister enabled her mother's addiction, which then in turn, enabled her own.

However, Halley wasn't about to admit that it was her fault either, though as far as she'd been able to trace back the roots, her mother hadn't started really drinking until after Halley had been born…

Had her mom been raped by Billy's dad? That was just a whole other ball of ugly that Halley wasn't ready to deal with.

"Look, Mom needs to take responsibility for her own behavior," Halley said. "Like you do, you know, when you're an adult."

"So now you're saying I'm not an adult," Caroline said. "Great. Want to tell me I'm ugly next?"

"Now that you mention it," Halley said. She tried to keep her tone light and teasing, but she knew Caroline wasn't having anything to do with it.

"Fuck you," Caroline said. "I suppose I won't see you out here this weekend to help, will I?"

"Given the kind of welcome you're likely to give me, why the hell should I?" Halley snarled in response. She picked up her dish and shoved it back into the refrigerator. "Look, I'm sorry that Mom has pneumonia. She'll be fine though. She's a fighter."

That had also been something that her mother had told them often. Halley was never sure if she believed it, given how much her mother lost herself in her drink.

Mom was a nasty drunk, though. Did she actually fight or stand up for herself when she was sober? Only sometimes.

"What if she doesn't make it through this time?" Caroline said.

Halley paused. She'd gone to the front door and had picked up her shoes, intending on going out and maybe finding a fight of her own.

That would mean a shabbier bar than the ones on Capitol Hill.

Hell, she might even go down to Georgetown. Call it a business expense.

"Mom's going to be fine," Halley automatically assured her big sister.

"And if she isn't?" Caroline asked again.

"Then your expenses go way down," Halley said. It was a smart-alecky reply and she knew it. She just couldn't care that much right then.

"You know what? Fuck you. Don't bother coming back for the funeral," Caroline said.

Halley pulled the phone back and stared at it. She wasn't about to call Caroline back. They'd just set each other off. Again.

Instead, she texted her best friend Taylor, seeing if she was available for "adventuring."

Luckily, Taylor called her right back, and they made plans for Taylor to drive them to Georgetown, to check out the scene there.

Maybe Halley's night was looking up.

CHAPTER 4

HALLEY GROANED as she rolled over in bed, reaching blindly for her phone which was buzzing with her alarm. She nearly knocked it off the built-in shelf behind the bed, but finally managed to grab it and swipe it off.

Then she fell back onto her queen-sized mattress. Shit. Her head hurt. She didn't drink that often, or that much. It just didn't make sense.

However, Taylor had been driving, and had seemed to intuit how wretched Halley had been feeling, and so had encouraged her to try some of the locally distilled liquor.

Halley had directed them to the bar where Victoria had last been seen alive. It was a small place, just a few tables. The bar mainly served the vodka they distilled on the premises, in the back half of the building.

She hadn't seen anything suspicious when she'd been there. No group of three guys. Or even two sitting back while one plied the women at the bar with alcohol.

While the bar itself didn't serve any food, Taylor had gotten Halley to order something from the food truck that stopped in a nearby empty parking lot. They did woodstove pizza. Halley had been impressed with how good it had tasted, the smoke adding quite a bit of flavor to not only the dough but also the cheese.

Still, Halley hadn't eaten enough to justify the amount of alcohol she'd consumed. Plus, she wasn't used to drinking hard liquor, just the occasional fruity cocktail or beer.

Damn.

The alarm went off again—seemed she'd just snoozed it. She finally shut it off and sat up, dizzy. At least the heat hadn't kicked in again, and she wasn't sweltering.

She assumed that she was actually still drunk. Was this how her mom felt all the time? Surely she must feel better than this.

Not unless she felt as though she needed to punish herself constantly…

Halley shook her head. No, she was not about to allow her thoughts about her mother and her family to get the best of her. She needed to pull herself together, get herself to the office, and start digging into the files and reports that Amber Lee had left with her.

Only the promise of coffee—and lots of it—got Halley moving from her bed and stumbling into the bathroom. She'd already thrown up what little had remained in her stomach, the pizza not coming back up as smoothly as it had gone down.

She stopped for a moment and glanced at herself in the mirror. Six feet tall, lean and athletic. Hours spent in the gym and the dojo had made a difference, and she could pass for ten years younger than her grizzled thirty-four. She was in too much pain that morning to fake her easy-going smile, the one that got people to talk to her, to trust her, even when they shouldn't. Her hair was frizzy, curly like Billy's and no one else's in her family. While it was still all brown, she kept expecting to wake up some morning with huge patches of gray, based on the stress in her life.

She'd at least stopped looking for a resemblance between herself and her sister Caroline, who resembled most of the rest of the family—short, plump, and blonde.

And dumb, though Halley tried not to state that with any regularity, or else she'd end up screaming it at Caroline on the phone at some point.

The hot shower helped Halley wake all the way back up. That was one good thing about her condo—they'd replaced the water tank in the basement as well as all the pipes just before she'd bought the place. So even though she was on the third floor, she always had great water pressure and was guaranteed hot water day or night.

She walked from the bathroom to her closet. A large built-in chest of drawers took up most of the back of the room. Her gun safe was bolted to the floor beside it.

Halley always knew that it was bad when she felt like reaching for her gun before she picked out her underwear for the day.

Should she start carrying it again? Or would the temptation be too great to just shoot the assholes who were raping women?

While the Texas defense—*Your Honor, he just needed killing*—might work in books and on TV shows, it didn't tend to work in the Seattle courts.

She left the gun where it was and slowly got dressed. Phoenix had had a few choice things to say about Halley always dressing in her closet once they had found out.

As Halley didn't bother to keep set hours—just going into the office when she needed to—she didn't feel any need to go there that morning. She had all of Amber Lee's papers at the apartment with her.

There wasn't much of anything in her fridge. She did have some instant oatmeal, that came with dried milk and fruit, in one of the cupboards, just for times like these. She added water, dumped it into a bowl, and set that in the microwave to heat while she began the critically important morning ritual of making coffee.

She always started with fresh water and grounds. She bought her beans from one of the local roasters. She hadn't moved up to getting bespoke blends of beans.

Yet.

She had an Aeropress for making the sweet nectar of life. The kettle was just about to the perfect temperature when her oatmeal was cooked.

Halley took one bite and nearly spit the oatmeal back out.

Yuck. Peaches. What the hell had she been thinking?

She fished the container out of the kitchen garbage.

Strawberries and peaches. She probably hadn't seen that it had peaches in it, just strawberries.

Damn it. She tossed the bowl out and forced herself to take a deep breath. She could pour her coffee into a to-go mug and go out to fetch herself breakfast. She needed to eat something, that was for damned sure.

Just as Halley finished adding the hot water to her Americano, her phone buzzed.

Who the hell was texting her that early in the morning?

Seemed that Phoenix was downstairs. And they had breakfast burritos.

Halley buzzed them up. She didn't much care what her neighbors thought of her regularly interacting with someone like Phoenix. While Halley herself wasn't gay, she didn't think anything of it. That wouldn't necessarily fit in with the values she'd been raised with, but fuck them.

She unbolted and unlatched her locks, then stood in the hallway with the door open. Phoenix came up the stairs, a vision in a dazzling white gown with a white fur stole and white gloves. They carried the paper bag on the palm of their hand, up above their head, like an old-fashioned waitress balancing a full tray.

"Good morning," Halley said. She was already salivating at the thought of greasy burritos made from pork sausage and cheap cheese.

"Is it really?" Phoenix said, giving Halley the once over. "You look a mess." They swept into the apartment. "Rough night?"

"Yeah, you could say that," Halley said. She wasn't concerned about the place being a mess—it never was. The bed was already made and in its place. Her files were still in the safe and her desk was clean as always. The only thing that was still out was the water kettle in the kitchen.

"And you're sure you didn't go to boarding school or something else that warped you completely as a child?" Phoenix said, looking around the neat room.

Halley just shrugged. It was one of the ways of standing out from her parents and her sibling. It had also been the only thing she could control while she'd been growing up. The rest of the house wasn't horribly messy, but it had never been clean.

Having a clean room to escape into had always been her solace.

And, yeah, maybe to make herself feel as though she was better than her sister and everyone else.

With an incredibly smooth, probably practiced move, Phoenix brought their hand around and presented the bag of breakfast burritos to Halley. "Fresh from Inez," Phoenix promised.

"Thank you," Halley said. She stopped before she reached for the bag, looking up at Phoenix. They were close to the same height in stocking feet, but Phoenix generally wore heels. "Why did you decide to treat me today?"

Phoenix gave her an enigmatic smile. "I have my reasons."

Normally, Halley would have just let that pass. This morning she might have still been feeling a little out of sorts. "No. Really. Why?"

Phoenix cocked one eyebrow at her, but Halley didn't budge.

"Fine," Phoenix said, "since you're being so obstinate. It was obvious to anyone who knows you that you were heading for a meltdown last night."

"It was obvious?" Halley asked. She blinked, surprised. She had kind of felt as though the black mood had crept up on her out of the blue. "Huh." She took Phoenix's offering and headed back to the kitchen. "Can I make you some coffee?"

Though Halley wasn't looking, she could practically hear the eyeroll. "Don't you have anything else?"

"Nope," Halley said. "Nothing nurturing. Just black coffee, as black as my soul."

"Well, you'll have to forgive me for not taking you up on such a generous offer of such darkness," Phoenix said.

Halley divided the burritos onto two plates and invited Phoenix to come sit down with her.

"I think I might have been okay," Halley said after she'd taken that first blissful bite of spicy pork and gooey cheese, held together with rubbery eggs. "But then Caroline called."

"How is your dear sister?" Phoenix asked. Phoenix hadn't met Caroline, or any of Halley's family. But Halley might have spoken a time or two about her sister and her mother, so Phoenix didn't have the highest opinion of them.

Plus, Phoenix had been there when Mr. Lewis and Dancer had told Halley about her bio-dad.

"Mom's evidently in the hospital again. Pneumonia this time," Halley said.

"Is it serious?" Phoenix asked, suddenly serious themself.

"Uhmmm, Caroline didn't seem to think so," Halley said after chewing and swallowing. Then again, they'd been much more interested in yelling at each other than actually communicating.

Phoenix nodded. "You might want to call the hospital and see if they'll tell you anything," they said sagely. "Because someone in your mother's condition, with pneumonia, then going to the hospital—that might be a deadly combination."

"Okay," Halley said slowly. Would it be worth it? Particularly if Caroline found out that Halley had gone behind her back?

Caroline already hated her. Halley didn't think one more infraction would matter all that much.

"I'll call the hospital after we finish eating," Halley promised Phoenix. "So are you just here as an angel of mercy? Or did you have something pertinent for the case?"

"The bars in Sodo aren't really where my people hang out," Phoenix said. "But I may have sent a couple of field agents out to get a feel for the scene there. Drag queens, of course."

"Of course," Halley said, nodding sagely, though she really wanted to giggle. Phoenix had developed an entire network of "field agents" and "spies" to bring them information about whatever case they had decided to help Halley with.

While a few of the people in the network were drag queens, many of them were more plain-looking folks, some variety of queer but hard working with regular jobs They were all thrilled to be helping solve cases, particularly when it came to crimes against the community.

Halley had never expected this turn in her career, but she had ended up taking on many more LGBTQ clients over the past six months as a result of working with Phoenix. She didn't always give them a discount—a girl needed to be able to feed her coffee habit, and those beans weren't cheap—but she did what she could.

"And what was the reception they got?" Halley had to inquire as she gobbled down the last of her burrito.

"Favorable, more or less," Phoenix had to admit. "The bars were actually happy to have some glamorous clientele for once."

Halley tried not to snort coffee out her nose. "I just bet," was about all she managed.

"The bartenders hadn't seen anything, of course," Phoenix said. "I think this gang of bad boys pay attention to the hunting grounds."

Halley nodded, suddenly sober.

It felt like trying to find a needle in a haystack. Supposedly this gang was operating out of Sodo and Georgetown currently, but what if they moved? And three of them made it so much harder to identify a pattern.

"We'll catch them," Phoenix assured her.

Halley nodded, wondering how many other women had been violated. And just what exactly it was going to take to stop this gang.

CHAPTER 5

Dalton couldn't help but gloat over their latest ride. Bitch had been difficult to break in. The drugs had hit her hard. She'd started stuttering, which was always a bad sign.

Had fucking Vern overdosed her?

But she shook her way out of it and had turned into a tiger, wanting to be taken hard and fast. Had liked having her hair pulled as he'd slammed into her, the pair of them kneeling on the dirty floor of the bathroom.

The stink of urine and bleach turned him on now, as did a bitch who was shaking and out of control.

He'd been first tonight, breaking her in. The others were going to get his sloppy seconds, as was only right. It had been his idea in the first place that they team up to find their rides. He'd been the one who'd gotten the drugs initially, though Rick had found a steady supplier now.

Dalton had started carrying a switchblade with him, ever since that crazy cunt had come after him.

The bitch he'd just ridden was still kneeling on the floor, shaking. She'd taken it good.

Dalton pulled the knife out of his pocket after he'd pulled his pants up. The quiet click of the blade as it flicked open sent a thrill down his back. His cock wasn't up for much, but he could feel it start to twitch as he leaned back over, closer to her.

She was on hands and knees, where all good cunts belonged. He got a good fistful of her hair and yanked her head back. Her eyes were glassy and her mouth was opening and shutting as if she were working some huge cock.

He ran the edge of the blade across her throat, though not hard enough to cut the skin. Just enough to scratch it.

Bitch didn't even seem to notice.

Dalton felt himself growing harder. Damn. It wouldn't take that much to kill her. She'd probably thank him for it, for ending her useless, pitiful life.

He felt himself get stiff at the thought, even though he'd just come really hard. He'd started fantasizing about it, about cutting some bitch's throat while he was riding her, feeling that death orgasm.

Not a little death, but a big one.

A sharp rap on the bathroom door made Dalton jerk back on his heels, stand up quickly.

The knock was followed by three short ones, a pause, then two more, so Dalton knew it was Rick wanting his turn.

Dalton put the knife away and sauntered out, feeling smug.

Soon, he was going to have to break out on his own. It was handy having the other guys watch his back. But eventually, it was going to have to be just him.

And some dead bitches.

CHAPTER 6

THE CALL to the hospital hadn't been that helpful. Halley had been able to identify herself to the person on the other end as family, reciting her mother's date of birth as well as her maiden name.

However, the nurse she'd talked with couldn't tell her much about her mother's diagnosis. Due to the alcoholism, and probably her mother's sheer stubbornness, the pneumonia wasn't detected for quite some time. There had been a large accumulation of fluid in her lungs, and one had collapsed before they finally got her in for treatment.

She was likely to be some time in the hospital while she learned to breathe again. The nurse wasn't about to make any sort of prediction about life expectancy on the phone.

Halley left her name and number, with instructions to be called if her mom got significantly worse.

When Halley got off the phone, she felt dizzy. Phoenix was still there, in the other room, sitting at Halley's desk and going through the papers that Amber Lee had left.

"Sounded bad," Phoenix commented, not looking up from the report they were reading.

"Yeah," Halley said. She sat down, taking a deep breath.

"I mean. I don't necessarily love my mom. She's been a drunk most of my life. Maybe when I was a kid I dreamed of her dying. But not, not really. I just can't imagine her not being there. You know?"

Phoenix pushed aside the paper they'd been studying. They'd taken their gloves off, a sign of intimacy that Halley appreciated. She'd only seen Phoenix's bare hands a couple of times, at her condo, never at the office or in public.

Phoenix's fingers were long, thin, and well-manicured. They looked delicate. But they'd also obviously been damaged and not healed well.

Halley had always wondered if Phoenix's hands had been broken during an attack, which had been the cause of the gap in their public timeline. She could find information about Phoenix, born Marc Tallent, and their schooling and performances. Then Marc had disappeared. A few years later, Phoenix had returned to the stage.

Rising from the ashes, as it were.

Phoenix always seemed to study their hands when they weren't wearing gloves. Halley wanted to ask if they were surprised by them, happy to see them, or disgusted by them. Perhaps all three.

Phoenix spread their hands out and kept their gaze on the nails instead of looking at Halley.

"My parents supported my initial career," they said softly. "They never understood that at some point, just being gay wasn't enough. I needed to make more of a statement. I needed to prove that I was here, to make an impact on an uncaring world. Like you, I never thought about them not being here. But then they were gone."

Phoenix looked up, their expressive brown eyes registering both surprise and sorrow. "Just like that. Of course, I've wished things had been different. But I also knew, and know now, that they never could be."

Halley nodded, her world starting to grow more solid again. "I'm going to have to go see my mom," she said after a few moments. If nothing else, to see her while she was sober, as the hospital was certain to make sure she wasn't sneaking in alcohol.

Unless Caroline was bringing it in to her. But her sister wouldn't do that, would she?

No, she was much more likely to steal whatever medications and drugs that she could. It wasn't Halley's job to warn the hospital of that, though.

"Think your mother would tell you the truth if she was on her death bed?" Phoenix inquired, their attention returning back to their hands.

"Naw. She's just as likely to try to bribe me into bringing her some hooch in exchange for the truth." Halley shook her head in disgust. That was exactly what her mom would try to do.

"I see," Phoenix said. They reached for one of the sheets of paper from Amber Lee's file and focused their attention on that.

Halley took the hint. "Find anything interesting?" she said.

"Did you know that these fitness watches have been used to solve other crimes?" Phoenix asked.

"Really?" Halley said, surprised and more than willing to be distracted by the case again.

"Really. A stepfather went to see his daughter. Surveillance cameras placed him leaving at a specific time. He claimed that she'd been alive when he left her apartment. However, the fitness watch she'd been wearing showed that her heart had stopped five minutes before he departed," Phoenix said, pushing the printout of the account toward Halley.

"That doesn't really help us, though," Halley said after

perusing the article for a few moments. "We already know that Victoria's watch was stolen, and that someone else was wearing it."

"What if they still have the watch?" Phoenix said.

"They might," Halley said. "But wouldn't they have done a factory reset on it? So you couldn't get any data from it?"

"True," Phoenix said. "But you might want to ask Amber Lee if she still has Victoria's phone."

"I'll ask," Halley said. "Anything else?"

"No, not really," Phoenix admitted. "Just evidence of a life cut tragically short."

Halley nodded. Phoenix much preferred the cases that Halley took that involved surveillance, finding out someone's dirty secrets. This was only the second time that Halley had taken a case with a death, at least since Phoenix had started hanging around.

"But I have a student," Phoenix said, rising. "And you seem to be well in hand."

"Yeah, thanks," Halley said. "I appreciate it."

"Of course, dear heart," Phoenix said. "I will let you know if my network hears anything."

"Thanks," Halley said. She let Phoenix out, then decided that she needed a fresh cup of coffee before she tackled the papers that Amber Lee had left with her.

However, she suspected that Phoenix was right. There wouldn't be much there, except evidence that Victoria was a vibrant, well-enough liked young woman whose life had been taken far too early.

HALLEY DECIDED to ride the bus out to Georgetown later that morning. There was a restaurant out there that looked interesting, that served all sorts of smoked meats.

She didn't bother with her big backpack, just a small backpack purse for her phone, her wallet, and other sundries. She didn't take her gun, telling herself that she didn't need it, didn't need the security of it.

She wore just a gray hoodie that Phoenix would have declared a fashion disaster, but Halley found comfortable on days like these. It was light enough in the face of the bright sunshine, but warm enough for when the weather changed (as it was sure to do.) Instead of jeans she wore purple-ombre leggings with comfortable sneakers, and a burgundy long-sleeved T-shirt.

Thankfully, the day was sunny. Maybe the worst of the spring rains were finally over. The cherry blossoms had long since finished their display, littering the sidewalks and the streets with dirty petals that even the deluge of April showers hadn't been able to wash away. The grass was sparkling green, and already growing too long based on the number of lawnmowers she heard as she walked through the neighborhood up to the light rail station. Leaves on the trees had lost their bright spring color, darkening into a deeper green for the summer, providing what was going to be welcome shade.

A larger than usual gauntlet of homeless were sitting outside the station. Halley sometimes would get a five-dollar gift card from the Starbucks nearby and drop it in one of their collection hats. She figured that was better than just giving them money. What they really needed was a roof over their heads, and she wasn't about to offer her place.

The stairs down to the platform, two stories underneath the street, were only half filled with people, as it was midday. Halley had occasionally made the mistake of heading toward the station during rush hour. She'd been astonished at the sheer volume of bodies all walking, shoulder to shoulder, down the stairs.

She always wondered at the half-airplanes dangling from the ceiling of the station. They made her uncomfortable. Airplanes should be whole. Only having the front part hanging there always made her wonder where the rest of the plane was, whether it was about to crash. The bright orange and red colors didn't help.

Wind blew down the tunnel, announcing the arrival of the next train as the speaker did. Halley stayed on the train through the underground parts of downtown, getting off when it first went above ground in Sodo. From there, she walked a few blocks to one of the larger streets and caught a bus out to Georgetown.

The bus dropped her off south of her intended destination, as she'd planned, so she could walk back through the neighborhood.

As far as she could tell, it was gentrifying. The houses in the area were still blue collar, with cars on blocks in the yards, interspersed with some properties that were better taken care of. However, the restaurants were starting to diversify. Instead of all ethnic, there were more yuppy places mixed in.

The area had plenty of warehouses back behind the residential blocks. Light industrial, though. Box trucks crept along the narrow streets that had no sidewalks, not big semis. It surprised her to see houses mixed in between the warehouses and more industrial parts.

The sound of traffic was constant. Smells varied as she walked, from exhaust to dirt, with the occasional whiff of smoked meats, the burnt popcorn smell of roasting coffee beans, or the yeasty smell of fermenting beer, depending on which storefront she was passing.

The gym that Victoria had visited that night was obvious, with a beachy mural on the wall. She noted the hours the place was open as she passed. She might have to come back at some point and interview players. It would probably be the easiest place to find Victoria's teammates.

From the sandy volleyball courts, Halley walked out of the quieter neighborhoods, closer to one of the main thoroughfares through the area. The smell of roasting coffee came from the converted train station across the street, a tall brick building that had an air of desolate elegance.

Halley passed by a couple of cafés filled with nomad digital workers, as well as an insurance shop, a pawn shop, and what looked like one of the original neighborhood dives, the windows filled with cheap neon and the smell of stale beer still lurking.

Up at the corner she found the distillery where Victoria had last been seen alive. Though she'd been there just the previous night, she still took the time to look around, since it had been dark and she'd been, well, not necessarily there to just do her job.

The building sat on a triangle of land. That explained why the front bar was so small. The backend was much larger. From where she stood, facing the distillery, to the left was a narrow gap between that building and the next. It was also fenced off, probably so that patrons couldn't go pee against the wall of the hair salon.

The distillery building itself was starkly industrial, though Halley would bet that it was brand new and just trying to fit in. Dark windows looked out over the street. There was a patio area that wasn't open yet, fenced off from the sidewalk with black wrought iron posts and a chain dangling between them. Large signs were posted out front about respecting the neighborhood and being quiet on and off the premises.

No such signs had been out in front of the dive down the street. Did that reflect different attitudes of the owners? Or different clientele?

While Halley wasn't used to drinking, she'd still been surprised at how quickly she'd gotten drunk. Was the alcohol they served at the distillery that much stronger? Did they have that many seriously messed up people leaving on a regular basis? Possibly.

Halley stopped on the sidewalk just in front of the entrance to the distillery, turned around so her back was to the bar, then closed her eyes.

Suppose someone had taken Victoria's fitness watch, and she'd come after him. Which way would he run?

Halley opened her eyes again. To the right was the start of the neighborhood, the street narrowing, with more buildings looming. To the left started the long bridge over the train tracks, heading back into the city.

If she was in a hurry, not thinking, running on instinct, she'd turn to the left, run up along the more open feeling street.

Halley went that way, trying to get a better idea of the area.

The sidewalk ran out almost immediately, so Halley was walking down the center of the small, enclosed street. After the large distillery, the next few places were warehouses, fenced in, with dumpsters out in front. More buildings appeared on the right side of the street, smaller older buildings that had probably been stores in kinder days, but were now covered with posters and graffiti.

The street wasn't too long. The adjoining street was busier, with a lot more traffic. If she was in a hurry, she wouldn't want to pause to try to run across it. Plus, there was a sidewalk here.

An old closed video store was on the corner, though the adult bookstore beside it was still open. It didn't have any obvious cameras outside the seedy looking door. Halley hurried by, irrationally afraid she might catch something just by walking too close. The rest of the short block was taken up with a convenience store. It appeared to be open, though there were solid bars on the windows, and the gate that was generally pulled across the door was just barely pushed to one side.

Around the corner, and up the street where Victoria had been killed. It wasn't much wider than the first street. Again, no sidewalks, so whoever Victoria had been chasing had probably been running down the center of the street.

Blank warehouse to her left, not even a sign to identify it. Security cameras, but only close to the large garage door. Chain link fence around an actual yard—the only grass she'd seen since she'd arrived in the neighborhood. No trees, though. There weren't any trees in this entire neighborhood as far as she could tell. A massage studio had taken over what had at one point been someone's house. No cameras there.

Halley stopped for a moment and recalled the report. Victoria's body had been found about halfway up the street. She'd been struck by a vehicle moving at thirty miles per hour. The coroner wouldn't guess how far she'd been thrown, but Halley bet it was quite a distance.

Had they been trying to kill her? Or just stop her? Or was it a freaking accident, had she been struck by a third party, innocent bystander who freaked when they realized what they'd done and had driven off in a panic?

If she went along with Amber Lee's theory, she would bet that the gang hadn't meant to kill her. That hadn't been their intent. They just hadn't realized how fast they were going. They'd all been drinking. They were hyped up on adrenaline and anticipation. Victoria's death had been an accident.

But if it was part of the same group, they were guilty of something. Probably drugging her, with the intent to gang rape her. Which was probably part of the reason why they hadn't bothered sticking around after they'd run her down.

Halley looked around the short street again. She could see why Amber Lee had called it awful. It wasn't a neighborhood, not like Magnolia or Capitol Hill. Whatever neighborhood had been there had been decimated by the warehouses and poverty. Only a few signs remained of what it had once been, like the nice house on the corner that was now a massage parlor.

Whatever surveillance tapes that showed any evidence were certain to be in police custody. And if they'd shown Victoria chasing after someone, Detective Branson would have been much more open to Amber Lee's theory of there being a gang of rapists.

Halley sighed. She still had a couple of "ins" with the Seattle Police Department. One was Dick, her former mentor. The other was Billy, her newly acquired half-brother. Who also happened to be Dick's current partner.

Did she want to see if she could talk to the pair of them? They weren't likely to listen, particularly since it wasn't their case.

On the other hand, she hadn't seen Detective Branson in a long while. Maybe he'd be more amenable to sharing what information he had, so she could pick up and continue the case.

Halley was going to have to write up her notes, damn it. Dictate them and get them transcribed. Just so she had something to hand the detective when they met.

More salt in old wounds.

CHAPTER 7

HALLEY SPENT most of the afternoon in her condo, dictating her notes so that they could be transcribed. Fortunately, the service she used had just had a client cancel with them, so they would be happy to turn her work around by the next morning.

She wasn't surprised to see Billy calling. Though he was only her half-brother, and he was technically younger, having been born six months after she was, he still checked in with her on a semi-regular basis.

Particularly if he'd found anything regarding the supposed suicide of their shared biological father.

"Hey," Billy said.

Halley could hear the frown from where she was standing. "What's wrong?"

"You free this evening?" Billy said.

"Sure," Halley assured him. "Where do you want to meet and when?"

"Old Charlie's," Billy told her. "Uhmmm. Thirty minutes? My treat."

"That works," Halley assured him.

Halley emailed her notes off to her service, then headed

out the door. The day had stayed gorgeous, and she had left her windows open all afternoon. While Halley liked her condo, she loved it when the leaves finally came in. She joked sometimes that she lived in a bird's nest, as just glancing out the window, all she could see were trees.

Rain was coming, though, probably later that evening. She wore a heavier navy-blue jacket that was at least rain resistant, and traded over for a cute pair of boots, though she kept on the purple leggings and long-sleeved burgundy T-shirt. Wind pushed at her as she left the building, as if hurrying her along. Lilacs were still in bloom and the wind carried their heady scent, bringing a smile to Halley's face as she walked down the sidewalk.

It was just a few blocks from her condo to the restaurant, so she took her time, walking a few blocks north, out of her way, before turning around and walking back south up the next block. She loved the neighborhood she lived in, despite how many of the older places had fallen prey to development, beautiful (albeit dilapidated) mansions torn down for hundreds of townhouses and pod-apartments.

The houses that remained were well-maintained and tended to have beautiful gardens. Many of the camellias were starting to fade while the roses were just starting to bloom. Halley smiled and nodded at the yuppies with their dogs, though most weren't paying attention to either her or their pet. Instead, they were too involved with their phones.

Dogs promoted a "healthy" lifestyle, not actual interaction with the animal.

Finally, Halley walked up to Broadway, one of the main streets through Capitol Hill. There was a pulse now to the street traffic, as commuters got off the train. She'd timed it perfectly for once, and so didn't feel like a salmon swimming up a hostile stream as she made her way to the restaurant.

"Old Charlie's" actually had a different name. It had been

a restaurant called "Charlie's" for decades, an old establishment on Broadway. It had burned down, reopened, then finally been sold off.

Halley didn't keep track of the new name of the restaurant. It had gone through two so far. For her and for many of the other locals in the neighborhood, it was still "Old Charlie's."

Billy was waiting just inside the door. "Hi, sis," he teased when he saw her.

"Hey," Halley said.

Billy looked tired, but not as exhausted as he'd been a couple months ago, when there had been a series of gang shootings in Belltown and it had been all hands on deck at the precinct. His white face actually had a bit of color to it. He wore his curly brown hair shorter than Halley wore hers. They were almost equal in height. When they went out to restaurants, most of the waitstaff immediately pegged them as siblings.

He wore a nice gray suit, possibly off the rack but then tailored to fit his long arms and broad shoulders. His shirt was a sunny yellow—maybe in celebration of the changing weather, but most likely because it had been the next in the rotation. While some cops wore fun ties, with cartoon characters that their kids had picked out, Billy always wore power ties in solid colors, this one a royal blue.

They didn't hug. Neither of them had come from families that hugged. While Halley had been trained to hug Taylor when they saw each other, that was about all the intimacy she had in her life currently.

Every once in a while she wondered about Chester, her ex, but that was the extent of her thoughts about him anymore. While she'd known intellectually she was better off without him, she hadn't figured it out emotionally for a while.

Peachy-yellow bright paint now covered the walls, and Halley could hear a Mariachi band playing on the speakers. Had Old Charlie's changed hands again? Must have. She could have sworn the last time she'd come here it had been a Thai joint.

A waitress led them to a corner booth. At least they'd kept the tall-backed booths, carved out of a dark wood. With the music playing and their location, it felt quite private.

Halley still missed the place across the street, long gone now, that had curtains you could draw over every booth, so you felt really enclosed and secluded.

"So what's up?" Halley asked after they'd ordered horchata and food. The waitress had brought over tortillas that were still warm, with three different varieties of salsa— red and sweet, green and somewhat spicy, brown and likely to burn your mouth.

"Nothing much," Billy said. He glanced out the window at the stream of commuters passing.

"Right," Halley said, laying on the sarcasm. "You would call and offer to take me out to dinner because you didn't have anything to say."

Billy gave her a sheepish grin. He leaned back in the booth and tipped his head back. "Maybe I just wanted something more normal for a while, you know?"

Halley did, actually. It was one of the things that she'd found she really enjoyed about not being a cop: the ability to go somewhere and fit in, to mostly feel normal in a social setting. It had taken a few years for her to get to that point, to get past the police force indoctrination.

Billy had been planning on becoming a lawyer. He'd only chosen law enforcement once their shared bio-dad had committed suicide.

Except that Billy was convinced that it wasn't suicide,

that it had been murder. He'd been gathering evidence for years to make his case.

Halley wasn't quite sure what Billy would do once he figured out who was the shadowy figure behind their father's death. Would he try to make the case stick, somehow? Take it to a judge?

Or would he decide to enact his own vengeance?

"So you want me to start so you can ease into your story?" Halley said.

"That'd be nice," Billy said with a tired smile.

"It isn't necessarily normal, you know, what I do," Halley warned him.

"I know. But it's someone else's case."

"Gotcha. So, I might be investigating a serial rapist gang," she said.

Billy snorted at her. "Another easy, slam dunk case, right?"

"Yeah, something like that." She filled him in on what she'd learned from Amber Lee, and how far she'd gotten with Victoria's death. "There's something there, though. I went looking at how many other reported victims match the pattern. There have been three so far, two in Georgetown, one in Sodo."

Billy nodded thoughtfully. "Won't be easy, not if there are more than one of them working together."

Halley rolled her eyes. "Tell me something I don't know."

"Have you tried tracing the drugs?" he said. "There really aren't that many cases with Rohypnol anymore. People have moved on to Ketamine and GHB."

"I know. I'm trying." That had been one thing that Phoenix had a better handle on, the illegal drugs that flowed in and out of clubs. They had promised to do some asking around on Halley's behalf. The problem was that there were too many drugs with too many names that all had the same effect: leaving a woman vulnerable to assault.

She didn't bother to mention that Phoenix was helping her again. Billy hadn't seemed that impressed with them. Then again, Phoenix had hit on him pretty hard.

That had made her giggle later on, realizing that if she had the right gender, Phoenix would possibly have been hitting on her as well.

"Was there any security footage of the crime? Or nearby?" Billy asked.

Halley shrugged. "I have an appointment to talk with Detective Branson tomorrow."

"Branson, huh?" Billy said, shaking his head. "Good luck with that. The guy's pre-retired. Barely does what he is supposed to do. Only has a few more months before he is gone with that thirty-year pension."

"Got it," Halley said. Chances were, the detective would be a dead end, but she already knew that.

"How's your family?" Billy said, though he knew that her relationship with her mother was about as good as the relationship he kept with his own. He'd moved back to Seattle without telling her when he'd be arriving. Then, he'd refused to see her.

She still lived in the mansion that he and his younger brother had grown up in, out on Mercer Island. Had kept the office where his dad had supposedly shot himself.

Halley had yet to visit the place, though she'd driven by it more than once when she'd been watching another house for a different case.

Seemed Billy's mom wasn't the type for inviting possible family over for Christmas either. Not that Halley was all that upset. Billy's mom sounded like a first-rate bitch, quite frankly.

"My mom's in the hospital," Halley said. "Pneumonia."

"Is it bad?" Billy asked.

"Who knows?" Halley said. She'd called the hospital again that afternoon and had tried to actually talk with her mom, but the nurse said she was asleep at the time. Probably still recovering from the DTs. "One of her lungs collapsed before they got her into treatment."

Billy gave a low whistle. "At least she'll be sober for a while."

"Yeah, I'm going to have to go see her, just for that," Halley said.

Billy nodded, but didn't push. Their one and only fight had been when he'd tried to convince her to just ask her mother about his father.

Halley wasn't about to confront her mother that way. Not when she was drunk. Possibly now that she was sober, though…

"And Caroline's still a bitch," Halley added. "Not looking forward to seeing her."

"More screaming matches?" Billy guessed.

"You got it," Halley said. Sooner or later, they'd apologize for the words they'd flung at each other like knives, hoping to hit.

Food came next, hot and spicy fish tacos for Halley and something bland and pedestrian for Billy.

"You sure you're my half-brother?" she teased when he made a face at how hot his gringo pollo carnitas was.

"I'm sure," he said sourly.

Halley had to admit they did look so much alike. And the DNA test had come back as a match. They shared about half their genes.

Finally, after Halley had demolished half her plate, Billy appeared ready to talk.

"I got a look at the original report of the crime," he said

without additional prompting. "When my—our—dad was killed."

"Thought you already had that," Halley said, confused.

"More than one report had been written," Billy said. He held up one hand. "I know. I know. More hinky stuff. But by the original officers reporting to the scene."

"So not the case notes, but something by the responding officers?" Halley said. "Wait. Was there some chain of custody issues?"

Billy grimaced. "Not really, no. But one of the responding officers was Officer Richard Murphy."

"Dick?" Halley said, putting it together. "My old mentor?"

"Yes," Billy nodded. "And my current partner. Did you know there's a pool going for how long I'll last?"

"Doesn't surprise me," Halley said. "Dick is also nearly pre-retired."

"True," Billy said. "And he's been in the system for so long he hasn't learned to change with the times."

Halley nodded. She remembered butting heads with Dick on more than on occasion. As he was her superior, she'd bitten her tongue and followed along, though she'd been proven right more than once.

Then there were the other times when his abundance of caution had saved her life. She couldn't forget that either, the one time they were clearing a crack house and he insisted they do it by the book, one room at a time, even though the reporting officers had said the place was clear.

It hadn't been. Halley had nearly been shot by a tweaker who'd been hiding in a secret compartment beside the tall fireplace in the main room.

Though she hadn't been a detective, she'd still admired the older officer, and had appreciated how he'd appeared to take her under his wing.

He'd told her later on it had been because he wanted to base a character on her for his novel.

It couldn't have been because he'd known the truth about her bio-dad. Right?

"Did you ask Dick about it?" Halley said. "About him being one of the responding officers?

"No," Billy said with a shake of his head. "I didn't want to call any suspicion to myself."

"Do you think he suspects that you're still investigating your father's death?" Halley said.

"Maybe," Billy said. He hung his head for a moment before looking back up at her, his eyes dark and blazing. "Yes. I'm sure he knows. But he hasn't said anything."

"Maybe he's waiting for you to bring it up," she suggested. Boys could be stupid that way, each waiting for the other to say something.

Billy shrugged. "Or I was assigned to him so he could keep an eye on me."

"That would imply a multi-generational conspiracy," Halley said. "Those are awfully hard to keep quiet."

"Maybe he volunteered to keep an eye on me," Billy counted. "The conspiracy goes beyond the police department, you know."

Halley rolled her eyes at her half-brother. "Dude. All you have to do is ask him if there was anything hinky at the crime scene. Or bring in the pictures and ask him to compare them to what he remembered from when he first arrived at the scene."

Billy bit his lip. "You know that things were changed, right?"

"Yeah, you showed me," she said.

There had been a trophy that Billy had found in a moving box when he'd arrived in Seattle. He swore he hadn't packed the box, but maybe it had been stuffed in among his things all along. It had contained his father's old winter coat, along with a trophy that his father had received from his company, congratulating him on a fine year in 1999.

Billy swore that trophy had been in the study ever since he could remember. Why had it been packed away? It hadn't been removed from there before his death. A picture of his father from three months prior had shown that trophy in the background.

Why had it been packed away with an old coat and some financial papers? Billy had never figured it out. Or how the box had made it into his possession.

There were other changes too, to the room. Subtle changes that showed up comparing the pictures while the body was still in the room to afterward, when forensics was trying to solve the case.

The filing cabinet on the right was no longer neatly lined up, but with a gap between it and the credenza, as if someone had shoved the cabinet out of the way, then pushed it back but not completely lined it up. Had there been something behind it? Or had someone been searching for his father's safe?

Books had been rearranged as well. And the trophies that lined the back wall.

Who had searched the room after the body had been taken, but before the police had released it back to Billy's supposedly grieving mother?

They knew that other people had been in the room when their shared father had shot himself. Both Mr. Lewis and Dancer—Kenny—had claimed to be there.

Who else had been in the room?

"So what are you going to do about Dick?" Halley asked. "You could grant him an exclusive, you know."

"A what?" Billy asked.

Halley rolled her eyes again. "Dick is forever writing that

novel of his. Promise him an exclusive to write your story for more details about the crime itself."

"Huh," Billy said, as if he'd never thought about it.

Of course not. Boys.

"Promise me you'll talk to him," Halley told Billy. "Don't go off on this deep end of conspiracies. You know that Dick is too old fashioned to have brought up anything to you about your dad. So you need to grow a pair and ask him about it."

Billy glared at her. "Grow a pair, huh?"

"Or whatever it is that cis-white boys do for actual courage," Halley shot back with a grin.

"You've been spending too much time with Phoenix," he said sourly.

Halley grinned at him. "I can't help it if my companions are so much more fabulous than yours, dear heart."

"Whatever," Billy said dismissively. Then he paused and gave her a serious look. "If you need backup, let me know."

Halley said, "Sure," though she had no intention of calling her little brother. Really, she could handle herself, with or without a gun. Besides, these guys were looking to debilitate a woman and rape her. They'd probably back down from any confrontation.

At least that was what she told herself until the next morning, when it was reported that a woman had been raped and then had her throat sliced behind one of the bars in Georgetown.

CHAPTER 8

DALTON COULDN'T HELP but laugh manically all the following day. Man, that bitch had never seen it coming.

He'd agreed to be last that night. Normally, he'd try to fight Vern and Rick. But he had plans, and it would be best if he wasn't first. Besides, he could tell that they were getting tired of him insisting on breaking in a bitch first.

Though sitting at the table with Rick, he could tell that his buddy just wasn't as smooth with the ladies, or in this case, the drunken whore barely staying on her seat at the bar.

They were back in Georgetown. They'd been splitting their time between Georgetown and Sodo. None of them lived in the area, which was one of the reasons why they'd chosen it. Plus, while the neighborhoods were gentrifying, it wasn't that fashionable, not by a long shot. Not as many cops were around as, say, in Belltown where all the gang violence and shootings kept happening. And it wasn't anywhere as cleaned up as Capitol Hill.

Besides, who knew what sort of freak you'd run into up there? Nope. Georgetown, and further north, Sodo, were much safer.

They'd gone back to the bar with the crazy redhead a

couple of times, but they'd never found a cunt who'd been as willing to play. Or maybe Vern was just gun shy.

That was also part of the reason why Dalton had backed down, letting Vern go first. Did he actually have the balls to do it? Even if he was botching his attempt at seduction.

Rick finally decided to go and save him, drug the stupid bitch before she wiggled off the hook.

The bathrooms in that bar weren't good. Instead of a small room, they were larger, with a few stalls. They couldn't take a chance on fucking her there, so instead, Vern took her out into the alley. The back door was just past the bathroom, so no one would see him leave.

Then Rick took off through the front door, walking casually around to the back so he could have his turn.

Finally, it was Dalton's time. He strolled through the back door, stepping out into the stinking alley as if he owned the place.

Which he would, shortly, though no one would know his name. He was still going to set his mark on it.

The bitch was on her hands and knees in the dark alley, vomiting next to the garbage dumpster. Appropriate really. Garbage in, garbage out. Her shorts were down around her knees, hampering her movement, exposing her cunt.

The guys had already loosened her up nicely. So Dalton just knelt down, unzipped, and had his fun.

But the real fun wasn't in the fucking. He knew that. No one else did.

Just before he came, he got out the knife. Flicked it open. Cunt didn't hear it, too involved in her crying.

Seemed that Vern hadn't given her too much, and she was starting to come out of it.

Good.

With what felt like a practiced motion, Dalton had leaned over and slid the knife across her throat, making sure to angle up and nick the jugular. Just cutting her throat open might leave her alive.

He wanted to feel her death throes while he was still inside her.

Man, it had been a glorious ride. He came his brains out as she shuddered and shook the life out of herself.

He was covered in blood, of course. Luckily, he'd planned on that. Had stashed a set of clothes in the back of the car. Stripped out of what he was wearing and took off, streaking naked down the alley to the car.

Sure, there might still be some blood on his hands and feet. But his shoes would be gone soon.

"Go! Go! Go! Go!" Dalton ordered as he slid into the back seat.

Vern started the car while Rick half turned in the seat to look at him. "Dude. What the hell happened?"

Dalton knew he carried a shit-eating grin to beat all. "Did her proper back there," he bragged.

"You what?" Vern said, sounding outraged, though he maintained the speed limit and didn't take his eyes from the road.

"I kept thinking about that bitch last fall, the ones you guys killed," Dalton said. "Remember?"

"Yeah," Rick said, sounding as if he had nightmares about it. Still.

"So I figured it was time for me to even the score. No, wait. You only have *half* a kill between you. I have one whole one, all to myself."

The next morning, Dalton still felt glorious. Even with the shouting and name calling the other two had done.

They couldn't believe that he'd actually ridden a cunt to death. They'd all talked about it. Dalton was the only one with balls enough to do it, though.

Fuck them.

It proved to Dalton that he was better off on his own, though, without them. Sure, it was going to be tricky, but he could pull it off. Better than those two assholes.

And he still had his prize from that redhead chick. He wore her fitness watch all the time, to remind him of when he honestly felt most alive. He had the knife that he'd used on the second one. Hadn't thought to grab something from her.

Next one, though. Next one he'd make sure to keep a trophy that was all his own.

CHAPTER 9

Halley felt sick to her stomach as she watched the story unfold. Poor woman had been roofied, raped by at least one perpetrator, then killed.

Had the sick fuck done it while he'd been inside her? It didn't bear thinking about.

But it meant that this group of "bad boys" had upped their game. Dangerously so.

Halley checked over the transcript that arrived at the shared office space, but as far as she could tell, nothing was missing. Detective Branson hadn't called and canceled.

It meant that there was a better chance that Victoria's death might be looked into more seriously, now. Particularly if toxicology could match the Rohypnol.

Halley had followed the police reports, and knew that a different detective, Detective Anderson, had caught the case.

Halley didn't know Detective Anderson, had never met the woman. She'd transferred into the department after Halley had left.

The detective's parents must have had a cruel sense of humor, though, as they'd named her Pamela. She tended to go by her middle name, Ellen.

Still, Halley could hear the jokes that were already being snidely hinted at by the news stations, who of course wouldn't call her by the name she wanted them to use.

Someone must have leaked her first name, though. Or maybe the PIO had done it, as Renee Bellweather, the lieutenant, didn't like competition for anything.

Halley was going to talk with Detective Branson first, then if she had to, she'd go speak with Detective Anderson.

After picking up the transcript at the office, Halley continued her way up the hill. Detective Branson had a fondness for Thai food, so they were going to the place near the end of Fifteenth Street. Halley liked their soup and spring rolls, plus they made the best black sticky rice and mango dessert.

It was still nice out—the rain the previous night had just washed everything clean then disappeared. Halley decided to take a chance and sit outside in the cool spring-like air.

Besides, she liked watching all the people in the street. She chose a table to the side of the door to the restaurant, so that neither she nor the detective could be surprised.

The deck was freshly painted, a nice dark red that didn't show food stains. The chairs were black metal, no cushions, but hers warmed up quickly as Halley sat there. Delicious smells wafted from the restaurant, and Halley nearly changed her order three times while waiting.

Finally, the detective came striding up. He was still in one of his infamous brown suits. Halley wondered if he'd found them on sale one time and had bought a dozen or so. His hair had thinned considerably since she'd seen him last, and lay as a silvered fringe over his long bald skull. His eyes were kind and he smiled when he saw her, as if he considered her an old friend or something.

"Good morning, Detective," Halley said, sticking out her hand to shake.

Detective Branson shook her hand with a firm grip. The skin was weathered and beat to hell. He must be doing some sort of outdoor work to have hands like that.

"Hello, Ms. Brown," the detective said. "I'm assuming this is some sort of official business, yes?"

Halley nodded. She wasn't about to lie to him and tell him that she'd called him out of the blue for a social visit.

"All right then," the detective said. "Let's do business after lunch then, shall we? And you can call me Trent until then."

"Halley," she said in return. "Have you eaten here before?" she asked as he took a seat to the side. That way, he could also watch the street as well as everyone entering and leaving the restaurant. Halley understood that and still carried that attitude from when she'd been a cop.

"I have," he said. "I love their mango sticky rice."

Halley smiled. At least it appeared that lunch was going to be pleasant enough.

Trent told Halley all the gossip in the department, who was having a birthday, who was finally retiring. He only had three months left before his own "permanent vacation" started.

Halley told Trent about the shows she'd seen lately, not just the drag queen reviews or burlesque shows, but the bands as well. And they shared the same taste in seedy police procedurals, though Halley didn't necessarily read them, but listened to them on audio.

After they'd finished off their sticky rice mango desserts, Trent pushed his dish aside and said, "So, Ms. Brown, what can I do for you today?"

Halley smiled. It was as good of a demarcation as any, that the pleasant part of the meal was finished and it was now time for business.

"There was a case six months ago now. Victoria Peters," Halley said. "Vehicular homicide."

"Yes, I remember," Detective Branson said. "Hit and run, right? Not much to go on."

"Victoria had Rohypnol in her system, according to the toxicology reports," Halley said. "Just like the newest victim down in Georgetown."

Detective Branson blinked slowly, as if he was recalling the information. "Wait. The rape/murder? That happened yesterday?"

"Yes," Halley said. She still had her notes in her backpack beside her. "Is there any chance that toxicology could match the drug being used?"

"Don't honestly know," Branson said. "Don't know if there's enough of a difference between manufacturers, or if each batch has its own signature."

"You might want to check," Halley said. "To see if the cases are related."

"But Victoria Peters wasn't raped," Detective Branson clarified.

"No, she got away before she could be," Halley said, determined. "And she was killed, probably chasing down her attacker."

"Is this about her fitness watch?" Detective Branson said.

"Yes. I've been hired by Victoria's sister, Amber Lee, to see if we can find her killers and bring them to justice."

Detective Branson grimaced. "Look, I'm sure that her sister, and you, mean well. But there isn't anything we can use from those reports from the fitness watch."

"What do you mean?" Halley said, confused. "The company that has the information will provide you with certified copies of the data. You don't have to believe Amber Lee's reports."

"Yes, but all it shows is that her watch was taken. You

have no proof that the same person who gave her the Rohypnol was the one who took her watch."

"I know that," Halley said. "But if the killer still has the watch—"

"Which you and I know is unlikely," Branson said.

"I realize that," Halley said, angry that she was still reaching for straws. "But there's been a pattern of these attacks in Georgetown. Three others who have reported a similar occurrence. Drunk and given Rohypnol, or some sort of chemical that left them with no memory of the event. All the women fit a specific profile as well. Young, lean, Caucasian, and athletic. More than one has reported her fitness watch taken as well."

"Oh," Detective Branson said after a moment. "There's been more than one? But can you prove that there's a connection?"

"No, I can't. That's what I'm asking *you* to do," Halley said, trying to not let her smart mouth get the best of her. "I want you to check the reports of the Rohypnol. See if they can be traced to a single manufacturer."

Detective Branson shook his head. "You know that any sort of report won't come back for months. Long after I'm retired."

"You're not retired yet," Halley couldn't help but point out. She didn't continue on or tell him to just, "Do your fucking job until then."

However, he probably heard the words anyway, as she was thinking them loud and clear.

They glared at each other over the cleaned table. Finally, Detective Branson nodded. "Fine. I will see if there's a report that can be run on all the victims, see if we can trace the Rohypnol. But I'm not promising anything. And I'm not promising that I'll meet you again for lunch." He paused, and put aside the detective for a moment. "Even if it was delicious."

Halley gave him her best easy-going smile, the one she faked so well. "Thank you for taking the time to see me today, though. I mean it. I do appreciate it. I know you're awfully busy. The case load never gets easier."

"No, it doesn't," Detective Branson said. Then he stood up, suddenly all business and hiding behind his shield again. "It was a lovely meal," he said, shaking her hand.

"It was," Halley said, standing, then watching him walk briskly away, down the street.

Would he actually try to connect the cases? Fill out a report about the drugs being used on more than one woman in the same area?

She doubted it, quite frankly. He was honestly pre-retired, and just counting the days until his pension started rolling in.

She knew she should drop it at this point. She didn't want to burn what few bridges she still had at the SPD.

But she still found herself calling her old mentor, Dick, seeing if he wanted to meet her for coffee later on that afternoon.

AFTER HALLEY GOT off the phone with Dick, she checked her messages and realized that Amber Lee had called.

Halley debated calling her back. She didn't want to. However, she suspected that Amber Lee would just continue to call her again and again until they spoke.

Halley walked into the quieter neighborhood, off of the busy street, and called Amber Lee at the number she'd listed.

"Hello?" Amber Lee said.

"Hi, Amber Lee. This is Halley, returning your call," she

said. The lilacs she was walking by scented the whole street. At the corner, a small brown and white dog was yapping happily, straining at his leash to get at the squirrel who'd just raced by. The sun felt good, warming Halley's back.

"Oh. Oh! Did you see the news? About the poor girl who was murdered in Georgetown? I swear that must be the same people!" Amber Lee said.

"I did," Halley said. "And I just had lunch with Detective Branson. I told him that the two cases were connected." She knew she had to give Amber Lee something, to show she was making progress on the case, even though she'd warned her client more than once that these things generally took time.

"Oh, thank you, thank you!" Amber Lee said. She gave a mighty sniff.

Halley knew the woman was already crying and tried hard not to roll her eyes. She certainly wouldn't cry over Caroline's death. Not many would, except her two boys.

"It's just so nice to have someone believe me, who is working to get justice done for Victoria," Amber Lee said in a watery voice.

"You're welcome," Halley said. "Now, I'm heading for another meeting about the case. Is there anything else you needed?"

"No, no," Amber Lee said. She sighed. "It's just—I feel so alone now. Without Victoria here."

"Okay," Halley said when she realized that the other woman was waiting for a reply. She kept her sigh to herself as she crossed the street. The buildings blocked the sunlight now and she shivered.

"Thank you, again," Amber Lee said. "Just—keep me informed. You know?"

"Yes, of course. Oh! Before I forget," Halley said. "Do you still have Victoria's phone?"

"I do," Amber Lee said. "We shared a phone plan,

because it was cheaper for us to have two together than each have our own."

"Can you drop it by the office tomorrow morning?" Halley asked. "Along with the charger?" She wasn't sure why she felt that she needed it, but she had learned to trust her gut long ago.

"Certainly!" Amber Lee said happily. "I'm looking forward to seeing you."

"Great," Halley said, though she didn't feel that way at all.

She sighed as she hung up, crossing the street and back into the sunshine.

She was a private investigator, not a surrogate friendship service, although this wasn't the first case where the client had tried to bond with her.

She supposed it was better than the ones who yelled at her and had to be forced to pay.

Maybe.

CHAPTER 10

Dick agreed to meet Halley at Gaybucks, at the southeastern end of Capitol Hill. It was one of the largest Starbucks still open on the hill, now that Roy Street had closed, the "faux-bucks" store that corporate had opened in the hopes of fooling the public into thinking it was a local, independent coffee shop.

Gaybucks was insanely busy, as usual. They had two lines of baristas taking orders, both of them falsely cheery. It always annoyed Halley. Baristas should be surly. Or grumpy. And certainly looking down their nose at your coffee choices.

She got herself a pour-over of the latest Nicaraguan bean they'd just started pushing. It would be over-roasted, she knew. But it would be better than the soap water that was their "home town" brew.

Dick was already waiting for her, sitting on a chair that was too low for him. He wore a gray suit, about the same color as Billy's but nowhere near as expensive. His yellow socks and boney legs stuck out from the ends of his pants, making his shoes look ridiculously large. He waved at her, then went back to sipping his coffee. Of course, he was seated in a corner, a cop habit, so no one could sneak up on him.

He still looked more like a retired professor than a respected police officer with decades of experience. Gray hair still completely covered his long, skinny skull, his strong jaw line was impeccably shaved. His thin lips sneered as he looked around the coffee shop. She couldn't wait to hear whatever politically incorrect thing he had on his mind at the moment.

Halley took a cautious sip of her brew when they finally handed it to her. A little spicier than she'd expected, though just as dark and over-roasted. There was a reason why she only ever got the holiday blends from Starbucks.

The seat on Dick's right was empty, and Halley folded herself over to sit on the low chair.

"What, did they make these damned things for kids?" Dick groused instead of saying hello.

Halley was used to his moods, however. "No, I think they're just some designer's idea of 'modern.'"

"Damned stupid if you ask me," Dick grumbled. "So, how are you? You look good. Better than usual."

"Thanks, I think," Halley said. "You look the same."

He grinned at her. "Yup. Not getting any older. Or at least that's what I've been telling myself this year."

"What, you got problems you haven't been telling me?" Halley asked. Dick wasn't a father figure to her, but she still looked up to him as her mentor. At the same time, she was still very aware that they were no longer on the same "side" as it were: she was a civilian and he was a cop.

"Nothing you need to worry about," Dick told her. "So why did you want to shoot the breeze with an old man this afternoon?"

"I thought you just told me you weren't old," Halley pointed out.

"Older than you. Wiser too," he said. "I know better than to stick my nose in places where it isn't wanted."

"Sounds like good advice, keeping a schnoz like that clean," Halley teased. "Unless you had something particular in mind?"

"Enough of your sass," Dick said. "Out with it. You have something. I can tell. You're worse than a cat who drank all the cream and blamed it on the canary."

Halley rolled her eyes. Dick was always trying new, snappy lines. She was certain that at least half the things he said came from dialogue in his book, the one he'd been writing for at least a decade.

"Two things, actually," Halley said. "First off, I know you're not the detective on the case of the girl found down in Georgetown."

Dick nodded warily. Halley knew she had to tread carefully, or the cop would come out and her buddy would disappear behind his shield.

"There was another girl killed down in that same area six months ago. And two others who have said that they were also given Rohypnol and then raped," Halley said.

Dick grunted. "So, what. You think there's a serial rapist down there?"

"Possibly more than one, a gang of guys working together," Halley said. She cringed as she said it, because she really had no proof whatsoever. Just the word of a drag queen, who she really needed to interview. She made a mental note to remember to ask Phoenix about Angel DeMure.

As she feared, the next words out of Dick's mouth were, "You got any evidence?"

She shook her head. "Nope. I do have a person who claims that it nearly happened to them. However, two other women have stepped forward with similar claims."

Dick pressed his lips together and nodded. "Doesn't prove it."

"I know that," Halley said. "But you need to face the fact that someone is taking advantage of drunk women down in Georgetown. Plus, there was one in Sodo as well."

Dick still didn't look convinced, so Halley pressed on. "They all have a similar build. Lean. Tall. Athletic. And more than one has had her fitness watch stolen from her as part of the attack."

"Don't know what you want me to do about it," Dick said slowly. "As you pointed out, I didn't pull the case. Anderson has it."

"Is she any good?" Halley asked.

Dick tilted his head from side to side. "Far as I can tell, yeah. Renee hates her cause she looks good on camera and might be bucking for that promotion Renee thinks is hers."

"That's why her first name got leaked to the press, isn't it," Halley said.

"Yup," Dick said with a grin. "But that might come back and bite Renee's big black ass."

Halley knew better than to try to discourage Dick or to get him to be politically correct. It wasn't his thing, not in the least.

"You said you had two things. What was the second one?" Dick asked after taking a large sip of his coffee, as if to fortify himself.

Halley wasn't sure she wanted to mention Billy to Dick. They were partners, after all. They had to rely on each other, make sure that they weren't walking into dark alleys alone. They needed to trust each other.

But Billy was in a dark place, darker than Halley generally went to. He needed to know if Dick was honest and true or not.

Besides, he was her little brother. She should take care of him.

"What do you know about the death of Mr. Evans? Billy's father?" Halley asked.

From the look on Dick's face, the question appeared to be completely out of the blue.

You couldn't fake surprise like that.

But then Dick's face went blank.

Whatever other emotions he had regarding that case weren't something he wanted to share.

"What are you talking about?" Dick asked, his tone low and verging on mean.

"Billy says his father didn't kill himself," Halley said. "You know that, right?"

Dick nodded. "Yeah. He's going to get himself in trouble if he keeps poking at it. You will as well. The case is over and done with, couple decades ago now."

Halley wasn't completely surprised by the warning. "You were the responding officer," she said, pressing.

"I know," Dick said. He sat back, as if he was suddenly weary. "It was quite a sight, for someone as new to the force as I was. I'd been handed an easy duty that week. Hadn't ever expected to be pulled into a homicide." He shook his head, his eyes far away but still hooded. "I'd seen a few ugly things by then. Woman beaten to death. Accident on the Interstate that left a whole bunch of mangled bodies behind. But this…yeah. It wasn't right. That rich house, all those rich people, and this poor sucker lying dead across his desk."

"Was it a suicide?" Halley had to ask.

"Looked like it from my viewpoint," Dick said. He turned to look at her. "I know there was some question after the fact. But he was lying on the desk, blood and brains spilling all around, and his hand was on the gun, lying there on the desk beside him."

Halley knew that was part of the problem. A gun shot, that close to the body, projected a lot of force. The victim's body should be skewed to the side, not flat against the desk, as the first pictures had shown. That had always struck both Billy and as Halley as just wrong.

The shot had penetrated Mr. Evan's right temple. As he'd been right-handed, that made sense. However, there was no gunshot residue on his hands. The medical examiner said it was difficult to measure due to the amount of blood everywhere.

Two of the people who'd claimed to be in the room at the time of death were dead. Both Halley and Billy were convinced there had to be at least one other.

But there hadn't been any sign of forced entry.

"So why didn't you bring it up to Billy when he got assigned to you?" Halley asked.

"Ancient history," Dick said, rolling his eyes. "Plus, I didn't put it together right away that this kid I was now babysitting had something to do with a case that I was the responding officer on, the week before I made detective."

That almost sounded true.

Almost.

There was something else there, but Halley knew she shouldn't push any more.

"You got anything else?" Dick said. "Anything more to ruin an old man's day?"

"Remember, you're not old," Halley said. "But you and Billy need to talk."

Before Dick could give her grief about "sharing his feelings," Halley added, "You two are partners. You need to be able to trust each other. Seriously."

Dick pressed his thin lips together and didn't say anything else.

Halley sighed. She knew she was right.

She also knew that hell would freeze over before either Dick or Billy would say anything to each other.

Hopefully, that wedge between them wouldn't end up with both of them getting killed.

CHAPTER 11

As Halley left Gaybucks to walk back to her condo, she called Phoenix and left a message, asking them to set up a meeting between her and Angel DeMure. Might as well call it an early night, as she hadn't gotten that much sleep the night before.

The afternoon sunlight was still bright, though clouds had gathered on the eastern horizon. Probably would rain later that night again. Halley liked this type of spring, as she had a lot more time in the sunlight. Not that she suffered from SAD—it just felt good.

Just as she turned off Thomas and onto the quieter street where her condo was, Phoenix called back. "Dear heart, your timing is perfect. Angel is here with me at the Double D, ready to give you an interview!"

"Great," Halley said, walking past her building and continuing up the street. "I should be there in just a few."

"Kisses, darling!" Phoenix said as they hung up.

Halley rolled her eyes. Phoenix was a performer, and there must have been an audience to play for. They weren't so over the top when it was just them and Halley.

More people were out on the sidewalk now, hurrying back to their houses after working in a cubical all day, going from one box to another. Halley knew she should be more kind, but really, she'd never been suited to that sort of job.

Although she was getting in enough exercise walking, she did need to get to the dojo soon. Tomorrow night would be her regular class. Hopefully she'd be able to make it.

The Double-D was split in half. The bar and restaurant were to the left of the door, while the stage was to the right, behind a roped off doorway so that only paying customers could see the fabulousness there.

The clientele at the bar were a mix of yuppies taking advantage of happy hour and LGBTQ folks looking to hang out with some of their own.

The bar itself always felt to Halley as though it had come from a circus. The broad counter was formed out of a half circle, like a stage. Golden poles rose up on either side of the tall, curved mirror against the wall. The shelves holding the bottles of liquor had bits of tinsel and sparkling lights hanging from them. Plus glitter, of course.

Phoenix was sitting on the far side of the bar. An angular looking person sat beside them. Halley assumed it was Angel DeMure.

Halley had to admit that Phoenix looked positively dowdy compared to Angel. While Phoenix wore a glittering green ball gown, with white opera gloves and their usual tiara, Angel was in a brilliant blue sleeveless dress and looked like a fashion model. Their dark skin was absolutely smooth and flawless. They wore a gorgeous brunette wig with long curling strands artfully arranged around their face. They didn't have gloves on, and their hands were covered in sparkling diamonds. Several bracelets hung around her elegant forearms.

Halley waved and walked over. The boy behind the bar

—Erik—had half his head shaved in a butch style, as well as beautiful blue eyeshadow. He wore a white T-shirt under a vintage brown and green men's vest. Erik nodded to Halley as she joined the others, already mixing a lemonade for her.

"Dear heart!" Phoenix exclaimed. They blew kisses in Halley's direction. "This is the fabulous Angel DeMure."

"So lovely to meet you," Halley said. "And what pronouns do you prefer?" She'd learned that just asking up front made things a lot easier. Some of the queens gave her a hard time for it, but it was just more polite than trying to guess.

"Oh, aren't you sweet!" Angel proclaimed. Their voice was a little deeper than Halley had been expecting. "She/her when I'm in a dress."

"Thank you," Halley said.

"And though you look like a little butch thing, you prefer the same, yes?" Angel clarified.

"I do," Halley said. "Phoenix said that you have a story to tell me."

"Oh, I do!" Angel said. "Particularly since now there's been an actual murder close to there."

Halley nodded. She hadn't forgotten.

Angel's story followed along the same lines as the story that Phoenix had already given her, though with more details about the cute bartender who ignored her, as well as a description of the boy who'd tried to get her drunk.

He was a white frat boy, in his twenties. Pudgy, with curly blondish hair and a hairline that was already receding. His friend, the one who'd tried to spike her drink, was a little taller but had that same frat boy look, with straight hair, though. Angel hadn't really gotten a look at the third one, but thought he was a bit darker than the other two, a brunette.

"I mean, really. Did he honestly believe that I was that innocent?" she asked, batting her eyelashes.

Halley wasn't sure. If Angel had been in full makeup, and wearing something revealing, she could easily be mistaken for a woman in a dark bar. Hell, she looked like a woman now. Only her voice would have given her away, and chances were, the idiot rapists hadn't really been listening to her in the first place.

"Is there anything else you can tell me?" Halley said as she finished her lemonade. Angel's story really wasn't much to go on. Three frat boys in a bar, drinking and trying to pick up girls.

"They didn't give off that serial killer vibe, you know?" Angel said. "They seemed, normal. Not creepy."

Halley nodded. That was one of the problems. Not all predators were obvious. Too many of them were hidden in plain sight.

"Do you think you could work with a sketch artist? Give us a better visual for these guys?" Halley asked. Taylor had a friend, Bridget, who Halley had worked with before, who had an ear for these sorts of things and was good at drawing out details. It wouldn't be solid enough to present at court, but it would give Halley something to work with.

Angel pursed her beautiful lips together. "I could try," she said. "But I don't know how good it will be."

"Anything would help," Halley assured her. "I'd really appreciate it." And she'd pay for Bridget's time from Amber Lee's funds.

"So, Amber Lee called me this morning. And this afternoon," Halley told Phoenix after Angel had sashayed away.

"Well, she's your client," Phoenix said with a mischievous smile.

"I distinctly recall you saying that she would be calling you," Halley said.

"And what makes you think that I haven't been talking to dear Amber Lee every day?" Phoenix said. "Poor dear is lonely."

Halley sighed. "That's true," she said. "I'm going to get Victoria's phone tomorrow. See if it can still sync with the watch. If whoever stole her watch didn't factory reboot the thing so that it wouldn't call home."

"If the attempted rapists took it as a trophy, I'd think they'd want it in exactly the same condition that they'd acquired it," Phoenix said.

"That was kind of what I was thinking," Halley said.

Phoenix gave her a sharp look.

"What?" Halley said.

"You are not going to do what I think you're going to do, are you?" Phoenix said sharply.

"What?" Halley said, confused.

"You're going to use yourself as bait," Phoenix huffed. "You are the right demographic. Tall, lean, in good physical condition."

"Oh," Halley said. She hadn't actually thought about going to a bar and playing at being drunk herself. She'd just thought she'd go to some bars in Georgetown with the phone, to see if she could get a hit.

"I hadn't, actually," Halley said slowly. "But now that you mention it—"

"No," Phoenix said. "You should not put your life on the line for a case like this. It isn't worth it."

"Are you sure?" Halley said. "Women are getting raped out there. Now, killed. Why shouldn't I be doing everything in my power to stop these assholes?"

"My people are getting harassed. Killed as well. All the

time," Phoenix pointed out. "Transwomen are especially at risk."

"But it isn't a serial killer going after them, is it?" Halley pressed. "It's the world at large. These are specific perpetrators. Who I can stop."

Phoenix gave an exacerbated sigh. "You're missing the point."

"Which is?" Halley prompted.

"People get killed all the time. You can't help everyone," Phoenix said. They modulated their tone, as if they were trying to sound light-hearted and not deadly serious.

Halley forced herself to take a deep breath. She did *not* want to start fighting with Phoenix, not how she fought with Caroline. Phoenix didn't help with every case, but in many ways, they were a partner to Halley, just like Dick and Billy were.

"You were the one who accepted this case," Halley reminded Phoenix. "If I do end up going trolling for these assholes, I promise you that I won't go alone."

"Correct," Phoenix said. "You will not go on your own. If need be, I will go with you."

Halley rolled her eyes. "The point is to be forgettable. To blend in with the crowd. And Phoenix, dear heart, you are likely to be remembered everywhere you go."

Phoenix opened their mouth, then shut it again. "You're right," they said after taking a sip of their champagne. "I am utterly unforgettable. People see me and want to be close to me, all the time. Like moths to a flame."

They looked over their shoulders, making certain that no one was paying that much attention to them currently.

"What if I went as Marc?" Phoenix asked quietly.

Now it was Halley's turn to open her mouth and then shut it again. She'd never actually met Marc, Phoenix's original persona.

Halley saw that Phoenix's attention had transferred to their hands. They were flexing and making fists in their white satin gloves.

"Hey, it's all right," Halley said. She knew better than to reach out and touch Phoenix. She still slid a hand closer, across the bar, so that it entered Phoenix's view.

"You don't have to do that," Halley said. "Not for me. Not for anyone. I'll get Taylor or Billy to tail me. You don't have to."

Phoenix appeared to realize what they'd been doing and slid their hands out of sight, under the edge of the bar. "All right," they said slowly. They took a deep breath and turned to face Halley. "I might anyway, you know."

"Only if you feel comfortable doing it," Halley said seriously. "I don't want to be responsible for more of your trauma. Can barely cover the therapy bills as it is."

Phoenix gave her a smile. It wasn't completely real, but it wasn't fully faked either. "Or the meds," they added. It was a joke they'd shared before, paying for each other's therapy and medications. Then they nodded. "Thank you. It was good for me to at least consider the possibility. I don't think it's time, not yet."

"I will be happy to meet Marc when it is time," Halley said, trying to put as much warmth into her voice as possible.

"It will be his pleasure, trust me," Phoenix said. They paused for a moment, then snuck a hand out from under the bar and briefly squeezed Halley's. "Thank you, again."

Halley didn't squeeze back, but did slowly slide her hand away, relishing the brief moment of touch.

Phoenix did *not* touch people. The closest they came was air kisses with their closest friends. Halley knew that they'd just shared an incredible moment.

And who knew? Maybe someday she would meet Marc.

As Halley was walking back to her condo, her phone chirped. It was Caroline.

Halley nearly let it go to voicemail. She actually was feeling better. She was no longer in such a dark place.

But her sister might be calling with news, so she answered.

"Hey, Sis. What's up?" Halley said, trying to stay chipper and positive though she could already feel her rage starting to build.

"Mom's worse," Caroline said. "She isn't responding to the antibiotics."

"I thought it was a viral pneumonia and she couldn't take antibiotics for it," Halley said, confused.

"She got an infection while she's been at the hospital," Caroline said.

Figured. If Halley actually cared that much for her mom, she might have tried to get her moved to a better hospital. Not that Spokane didn't have good healthcare, but surely the doctors here in Seattle would be better.

"Doesn't it take a couple days for antibiotics to work anyway?" Halley asked, crossing the street to avoid the huge dogs straining at their leashes on the other side.

"The doctors are worried," Caroline insisted.

Yeah, right. The doctors wouldn't have come out and actually used those words. Caroline was worried and wanted some sympathy.

"I'm not coming out to Spokane tonight," Halley said. "I'm in the middle of a case. But I'll call the hospital again tomorrow, see if I can talk with Mom."

"I thought you'd been going behind my back that way," Caroline said.

Halley rolled her eyes and took another deep breath. "Look I'm not going behind your back. She's my mother too. I just wanted to see how she was doing."

"You've never cared before," Caroline sneered. "It's always been my job to take care of her. My job to clean up her messes."

"You could move her into a home," Halley said. "We've talked about this. She isn't working anymore. She needs more care than you can give her. We should put her someplace."

"What, shunt her off like she's no longer important?" Caroline said. "Like she's no longer our mother?"

From the way her tone was creeping up, Halley knew that Caroline was working her way into a huge fit.

"I don't want to fight with you," Halley said, surprised to find out that the words were true. "I really don't, Caroline. I know you're worried about Mom. I am too. But she's in good care at the hospital right now."

"Not if they were the ones who gave her that infection," Caroline contested hotly.

"Do we need to move her to a different hospital?" Halley asked. "I'm serious. If you don't trust that place, then let's find another one."

"I'll end up doing all the work," Caroline whined.

"I can help," Halley said. "I can look at all the hospitals in the area. See which one is the highest rated."

"She's at the highest rated hospital in the area already," Caroline said. "Look, I don't want to move her."

"Then what do you want to do?" Halley asked, trying to keep her tone reasonable as she turned up the street with her building.

"I...I don't know. I just wanted to tell you the news," Caroline said, sounding deflated.

"And I appreciate that," Halley said. "I really do. I'm glad you called and let me know how she's doing. How are you doing?"

Halley regretted the words as soon as they came out of her mouth.

Caroline started on her usual rampage about what an idiot her immediate boss was, how no one appreciated her at work, not really, how expensive the kids were, how that deadbeat of an ex-husband wasn't paying child support, and so on.

"You were right to stay single," Caroline said. "Be on your own, in your work and in your life."

Halley blinked with surprise. That was a new one. Normally, Caroline berated her for not having a husband or at least a boyfriend, as well as a couple of kids with more on the way. Plus, she'd never thought that Halley did any good working as a private investigator, claiming that Halley's work wasn't important.

"I've always thought so," Halley said, though she knew she was lying. She'd love to have a real boyfriend, a partner to help her get through the rough times.

Like these.

"Okay, I'm back at my condo," Halley lied. She'd not bother going into the building as she'd listened to Caroline rant, but had continued to walk around the block. Twice. She was just starting down her block for the third time. "I'll talk with you tomorrow, see how you and Mom are doing. Sound good?"

"Yeah," Caroline said. She sounded tired, as if being nice had taken a lot more out of her than a fight would have.

"She's going to be fine," Halley reassured her. "Mom's a fighter."

"I know you're lying," Caroline said. "But that's okay. Sometimes we just need to keep lying to ourselves to get through the day. Talk with you tomorrow."

Halley looked at the phone, surprised that Caroline had disconnected that quickly.

There was probably something else going on in Caroline's life. A new boyfriend, perhaps?

Halley could only read the echoes of the disaster in the distance. She had no desire to put herself in harm's way, as it were.

But she knew in her gut, just as she knew these assholes weren't finished raping and killing women, that she was going to be headed back to Spokane sooner than she expected.

Halley hadn't been able to reserve the smaller conference room at the shared office space. So she texted Amber Lee and made arrangements for them to meet at one of the nearby coffee shops on Fifteenth Avenue.

As opposed to Gaybucks, the baristas were properly surly, standing behind their counter, playing discordant modern music and probably bragging about how obscure their recent vinyl record acquisition was. Pastries filled the cabinet next to the register, all appropriately gluten- and taste-free.

Halley got herself a pour-over of their latest roast, a Sumatran that while dark, wasn't bitter. She found herself standing with her cup in her hand, just sniffing, getting high off the aroma. She might have to buy some of these beans. The rich smell filled her soul.

Amber Lee came in while Halley was still standing there. The Texas woman looked a little lost. Compared to the neckbeard hipsters and wannabe hippies, Amber Lee appeared like a brighter light, although clueless.

Halley raised a hand from her mug of divine nectar and waved, so Amber Lee would see her standing there. There were open seats at the bar beside her, so Halley just moved sidewise and took one.

That way, she'd be closer to the coffee. Delicious wafts of various roasts drifted her way.

The chairs at the end of the bar were stools that spun. Halley found herself pushing herself from side to side like a kid as she waited. The floor was concrete and highly polished, though there were a few artistic stains in the corners. A wall to Halley's left separated the shop into two parts, with the baristas on one side and their clients sitting, grateful with their indulgence, on the other. The opening in the wall had an elegant, high arch, all that remained of the original building.

"Did you see that artwork?" Amber Lee said in a hushed tone as she came up. "Lord almighty."

Halley hadn't actually paid any attention to the art on the walls. It was probably from a local artist. The coffee shop participated in the monthly art walks through the neighborhood.

The picture frames were at least a foot square, mostly holding white matte. The actual artwork was a three inch strip that ran across the center. It was primarily red and green ink drawings. At first glance, it looked like large red, green, and white leaves and vines. It was only after her second look that Halley realized it was actually vaginas, penises, and breasts.

"Someone thinks its art," Halley commented dryly. "You could buy a piece. They're all for sale."

Amber Lee looked much more horrified than Halley had anticipated.

Before Halley could apologize, Amber Lee started chuckling. "You know, that's exactly something my dear Victoria would have said, teasing me about such things."

She climbed onto the stool beside Halley. Only then did Halley realize that these seats weren't necessarily going to be comfortable for shorter people, or for people who had stubby legs.

Well, she hadn't planned on this being a long meeting, so maybe it was for the best.

"I brought you Victoria's phone," Amber Lee said, as if she recognized that this wasn't the best time or place for a chat. She placed a giftbag on the counter between them. It was made from stiff paper with gold and pink stripes down the outside. "Her phone's in there, along with the charger. The gift card has her password on it." She took a sip from her own cup of what looked like hot chocolate, complete with whipped cream.

At least Halley knew they made a good hot chocolate here, so she didn't grimace at it. Much.

"I went through all the apps last night, making sure they were still connected," Amber Lee said. She sniffed, and her eyes grew watery. "It wasn't easy. I kept expecting her to pop up over my shoulder and demand to know what the hell I was doing."

"I know this is hard for you," Halley said. "And we can't be certain if the phone will help at all. Chances are, whoever took her watch is long gone. And they didn't keep the watch as it was, they probably did a factory reset on it, wiping all the data."

"I know," Amber Lee said despondently. She reached for her purse and pulled out a cloth hanky, then delicately wiped her nose with it. "And I know you can't promise me anything, can't guarantee that you'll be able to bring Victoria's killer to justice. It's just such a relief that something is being done, though."

Halley nodded. "You'll get through this," she reassured

the other woman, though she felt pretty far out of her depth. She occasionally had to console clients, particularly when they found out that their spouse was cheating. Most of the time, though, like Amber Lee, they were relieved that someone had agreed to do something.

"What else have you learned?" Amber Lee asked brightly as she composed herself.

"I don't know if it's possible to determine the manufacturer of the Rohypnol," Halley said. "But I've asked Detective Branson to look into it, to see if the other cases we know about have the same signature."

"Ooh!" Amber Lee said. "I never thought to ask about that!"

"I'm not a chemist," Halley warned. "I don't know if it's possible. But I figured it wouldn't hurt to try."

Amber Lee took another sip of her drink. "Is there anything else you can tell me about? It's so much nicer working with you than with the detective! He wouldn't tell me anything."

Halley nodded. She understood Detective Branson's reticence. It had been an open case.

Plus, give Amber Lee an inch and she'd end up in your house baking brownies for you. They'd probably be good ones, too.

"There's another angle I'm investigating," Halley said. "Another person who someone tried to get drunk, then place Rohypnol in their drink."

"Really?" Amber Lee's eyes grew big. "Tell me!" she breathed out.

Halley realized that this woman lived on gossip. "I can't divulge my source," she said firmly. "I don't want to compromise their safety."

"Oh, I never thought of that! Of course, of course," Amber Lee said.

"I will arrange for this other person to work with a sketch artist, though, to see if we can get a better idea of what these people look like," Halley did add, as she was going to charge Amber Lee for it.

"Wow," Amber Lee said. "Like from the police department?"

"No, a friend of mine, though I've used her before on cases," Halley said.

Amber Lee sighed. "Victoria would have so loved this. She would have found it exciting to be involved with a case like this."

Halley nodded. "Hopefully we'll be able to find something that we can use. But I want to emphasize to you that even if we find these serial rapists, we may never be able to tie them to your sister's case."

"I understand," Amber Lee said. "But in my heart of hearts, I know that they're one and the same."

Halley wasn't sure if she felt the same way or not. However, it was good that her client believed that. So if she solved the one crime, her client would be satisfied.

And Halley would have made Seattle and its environs a safer place.

***

BILLY CALLED after Halley had said goodbye to Amber Lee and was walking up to the shared office space.

"What the hell did you tell Dick?" he demanded.

"Just that the pair of you needed to talk," Halley said, startled. "About how he'd been at the crime scene of our father's death."

"He just ripped me a new one," Billy fumed. "Said I needed to 'keep my nose clean' if I knew what was good for me."

"Did he actually threaten you?" Halley asked. She'd stopped walking in the middle of the sidewalk and made herself step onto the boulevard to let the woman with her SUV-sized stroller past.

"No, he knows better than that," Billy said. "But he's really upset about it."

"Yeah, I know," Halley said. "I could tell that. There was something off about the case. But he isn't about to tell either you or me about it."

"So what did he say to you exactly?" Billy asked.

Halley sighed and closed her eyes. She'd always been good at this sort of thing, remembering exact words and tone of voice.

"I told him that you believed that your father didn't kill himself. Dick said you were going to get into trouble if you kept poking at it. The case was over and done with. Then he talked about what he'd seen, how the body was lying across the desk, the gun underneath the hand. I asked why he hadn't told you about it, and he said it was ancient history," Halley said.

She opened her eyes to the bright sunny day again. A semi of baked goods started backing up in the grocery store parking lot next to her, the beeping annoying enough that she started walking again to get away from it. "Now, I don't want you going off onto another paranoid tangent. But I think Dick was hiding something."

When Billy didn't respond after a few moments, Halley looked at her phone to make sure they hadn't been disconnected. "Talk to me," she said finally.

"Okay, you're just going to call me paranoid again. But I thought the same as well. That Dick is hiding something. He knows more about what happened than he wants to say," Billy said. "Maybe about the body being staged or something."

"He seemed to feel sorry for your dad. As he put it, that rich house and all those rich people and that body on the desk." Halley remembered at the last minute to not call Billy's father "that poor sucker."

"All those rich people…" Billy's voice trailed off. "It was just my mom. She was the only one in the house. She'd come back from an opening at the art museum. She said she was alone."

"Do you believe her?" Halley asked.

"I thought I did," Billy said. "I thought she wouldn't lie to me about this. Now, I don't know. It's always been difficult to get the truth out of her, you know?"

Halley snorted. "Tell me about it," she said. She wasn't certain if she'd ever get the truth from her own mother, even if she was lying on her deathbed.

"But she always swore she was alone," Billy said. "That she discovered the body."

"Who else would have been there?" Halley asked. "Because yeah, Dick did say, 'all those rich people.' Was he talking about other people who were in the house when he arrived?"

"We know that Mr. Lewis and Kenny were there when Dad was killed," Billy said. "His business partner, Marti Coleman, has a tight alibi, not that anyone really looked that hard at him. It was a suicide."

"I know that he supposedly killed himself because of the business, right?" Halley said. "He was in debt."

"Yeah," Billy said. "Mom borrowed money from her family to pay it off and hush it up."

"Was your mom there when Dad died?" Halley said. She crossed the street so she could walk in the sunlight again. "I know she went to the show."

"She couldn't have been there," Billy said. "I checked that she was at the show until it closed at nine PM. It takes time to drive from downtown Seattle to Mercer Island. She didn't call 911 until ten-ten."

"And she swears she didn't walk in on anything," Halley said.

"I've never asked her," Billy said.

"Maybe you should," Halley tried to suggest gently.

"Yeah, all right. I'll go talk with my mom," Billy said. He sounded like a recalcitrant teenager. "But you need to talk with yours as well," he added.

"I know," Halley said. "I was figuring I might go out there in the next day or so. She got an infection from being in the hospital."

"Figures," Billy said. "Gonna die if you don't go, same if you do, though."

"Our modern life," Halley said. She paused, then had to ask, "You and Dick going to be okay?"

"Yeah, we're fine," Billy said after a few moments. "We'll go to the range tomorrow. Shoot up stuff. Shoulder-to-shoulder bonding. You know."

Halley smiled. She did know. She always felt better herself when she drove out to the range and spent some time peppering targets with bullets. Maybe later. Tonight was her lesson at the dojo. That was going to make her feel better as well.

"Talk with you later," Halley said. "Take care of yourself. Keep yourself safe."

"You too," Billy said.

Halley just stood there for a moment after she hung up with her half-brother. It was weird to have a connection like that. She decided that she was glad she'd talked with Dick. There was something off in his report of the scene.

Something about all those rich people.

Halley shrugged and started walking again, heading to

the shared workspace. She had another client to meet closer to noon. While it was nice to have Amber Lee paying for so much of her time currently, she needed to keep hustling, keep a pipeline of new clients coming in.

No rest for the wicked. Or even the semi-wicked.

CHAPTER 13

Halley was happy to take on another plain surveillance case after all the intrigue with Billy and Amber Lee. It felt cleaner, in a way. For her PI license, she specialized in criminal investigations. While cheating spouses wasn't a criminal offense, they were still her primary income.

She had contacts with other PIs, including a couple who did forensic accounting. She'd shoot herself if she had to spend her days tied to a computer checking numbers. Then rechecking. Then rechecking, as her dyslexia would make a hash out of anything she was working on.

It felt good to be on another case. She spent part of the afternoon using the computers in the office, upstairs in the shared space. While there were private offices (that cost much more) Halley merely rented a desk and a terminal from the shared space.

The shared office space was composed of eight cubicles, four on a side. The walls weren't that high, so she could comfortably see over them as she walked down the aisle between them. Two printers and all their accouterment lived on the far wall—one black and white, one color. A scanner and fax shared the cabinets there.

More than one safe was bolted to the wall there as well. People rented space in the safes, just like they rented desk space. Halley didn't trust her notes here, and instead, always took them home with her. It was a chain-of-evidence thing as far as she was concerned. Either her notes were with her or in her safe back at her apartment.

Tall window frames filled the outside wall, painted white, like the rest of the room. The cubicle walls were a dark gray, and the tough industrial carpet was a light gray, giving the room an airy touch. Beautiful crown molding with sunflowers in the corners separated the tall walls from the ceiling.

Halley was lucky that afternoon and got a desk next to a window. Though officially all the desks were open at all times, there were people like Luther who had preferred seats. He always sat in the middle cubicle against the inside wall. He did medical transcription, something Halley hadn't even realized was a job until she'd met the man.

She sat down, carefully putting her coffee on the desk so she wouldn't spill it, then made a few quick notes for herself about the new case. It hadn't come directly from Phoenix, but from the grapevine.

The new client was an older man who had married a much younger man, a May-December romance, with over twenty years separating them. They'd been happy for quite a few years, but now the older man was worried that he wouldn't be enough for his younger lover.

Halley first looked up Chet, the older man, seeing what she could find. She'd slowly learned that she really needed to investigate her clients as well as whoever they had her tailing. More than once the person who had hired her had more things to hide and was just looking for dirt on their spouse.

However, Chet appeared to be an upstanding citizen in the gay community. Had a funny Facebook feed with pictures of their dog, frequently begging for food, as well as kisses blown to his husband.

Red, as the younger husband was known, though his real name appeared to be Martin, also had posts of their dog and blown kisses. However, he wasn't on social media as much as Chet. Or he was hiding his posts, only showing them to friends.

They had quite a few shared interests, but Red followed a lot of musicians and bands. That appeared to be where their interests diverged. They didn't share a single "like" across their musical spectrum. In fact, music didn't appear to be that important to Chet.

Halley had a good sense of Red's schedule. She decided to tail him that evening, after work, just to get back in the habit of doing that sort of thing.

She left word for Bridget and gave her Angel DeMure's contact information, letting her know the type of sketch that Halley was looking for. Then she spent time answering the rest of her email, deleting scintillating offers such as free cheap coffee from a shop she no longer frequented (and she could have sworn she'd unsubscribed from their mailing list), a newsletter from a lesbian literary society that she'd probably been shamed into contacting, news from her alma mater UW, as well as an actual email from a client, letting her know that the court case was over and she'd won, thanks to Halley's work.

Halley didn't accept email inquiries from potential clients. It would be far too easy for people who weren't serious to try to reach her. She did have an appointment calendar that she kept on her website, so people could schedule a free consultation with her.

It had cost her a little bit of money, but she'd gone ahead and gotten a more customized calendar for her website. It always showed all slots within two weeks from the current date as booked. That way, she never had to worry about someone making an appointment while she was currently in the middle of something. She had a couple of appointments for new clients the following week, and three more for the week after that.

Business was a little slow, but that was okay. It had been nuts over the holidays, as usual, spilling over into February, which had not been usual. Halley actually didn't mind having a bit of a breather now in May, though she anticipated that as the temperatures rose, so would tempers, and she'd be busy again come summer.

Besides, that gave her more time to look at Amber Lee's case. She caught up on the latest developments in the most recent murder—a young career woman, just out of college, named Diana. She'd been out for a good time with the girls, but they'd had a fight. The coverage lingered over her friend's tearful remorse that they hadn't stuck together.

Halley didn't wish that on anyone. She knew that while the girl shouldn't blame herself for her friend's death, she always would. Police didn't have any suspects. No one had an artist's sketch because no one knew who had done it. They hadn't opened a tip line, not a special one, not yet. They just gave the usual number for all incoming calls.

No one had seen anything. No one had done anything. Just another drunk girl who got taken advantage of. Such a shame, move on.

It pissed Halley off that guys could go out drinking and it would just be excused as "boys will be boys." While if had something happen to a woman, well, it was her own fault, somehow.

She hated the double standard. Hated, too, that this case made her feel unsafe.

Maybe she should go and get her gun, carry it with her just for a while…

No. Not unless she actually was going to put herself out as bait.

Hopefully, the case wouldn't cause her to do that.

But she doubted that her luck would remain that good.

———

HALLEY GOT off the bus south of Seattle University, following Red. She'd been on the same bus with him since he'd left his office downtown. He'd told Chet that he was meeting some friends after work for drinks. Chet was afraid that this was code for meeting a new lover.

Red hadn't seemed like someone who was meeting a lover, though. He spent his entire bus ride standing close to the front, listening to music and singing along.

There was something intense about Red's singing. He wasn't just humming along or bobbing his head. No, he mouthed every single lyric, as if they were songs he'd written himself.

In compliance with his nickname, Red's hair was a nice, light auburn color, probably natural, based on the color of his eyebrows and beard. Though he was the same age as Halley, thirty-four, he had white streaks coming down the corners of his red beard. His gray-green eyes seemed full of intelligence. He'd stood on the bus, allowing other people to have seats. He constantly stepped from one side to the other, being considerate.

Maybe that outflow of compassion included love for another man in his life, but Halley didn't see that in Red. There was something else going on here.

Halley didn't put it together until she saw Red skipping up the steps to the Flying House headquarters. She took a couple of quick photographs, trying to line up his profile with the sign, getting them both in the photo at the same time.

Other men were also starting to trail into the building, separating themselves out from the constant stream of students heading back from classes to their shared housing.

This was where the Seattle Men's Chorus practiced. Not the entire chorus, just a section or so appeared to be arriving that evening.

Did Chet know that Red was a member? Or was this just tryouts? Halley would have to find out.

Halley turned away, a little disappointed that the case had been so easy to solve. She'd still do her due diligence, follow Red for a few more days to see if there was an actual other person he was involved with.

She doubted it, however.

Chet had been right. It was a type of adultery. Red loved music, and had snuck out behind Chet's back in order to start performing.

Halley had just enough time to pick up a quick burrito from a nearby taco truck before she boarded the bus again, this time heading north and then west, toward the water, to her dojo. It was time for her to re-engage with one of her first loves as well.

HALLEY WAS SLOWLY WALKING BACK to the bus when her phone rang again. She was feeling every single one of the falls she'd done that evening. She was really looking forward to a long hot soak in her tub before tumbling to sleep.

She nearly didn't answer—the number was an unknown Spokane number.

Then she saw the word *hospital.*

"Hello?" Halley said, swiping it on.

"Is this Halley Brown?" inquired a soft feminine voice on the other end.

"It is," she said.

"This is Nurse Edgar, from the hospital. I'm calling about your mother," she said.

Halley froze, waiting for the worst.

"Your mother has been steadily declining," the nurse said clearly. "We are having difficulties getting her oxygen levels back up to normal. If you can come out, you should."

Halley took a breath, not realizing that she'd been holding it. "I can be there in a few hours," she assured the nurse.

"I'm not sure that's necessary, but it might not be the worst idea," the nurse said.

"All right, thank you for calling me," Halley said.

She hung up, then debated calling Caroline. Why had the nurse called her and not Caroline? Unless the nurse had called Halley first, and was only now contacting Caroline.

Sure enough, just as Halley made it to the bus stop, Caroline called.

"You've got to get here. Now," she said.

"I'm on my way," Halley replied.

"You need—wait, what?" Caroline said. "I don't have to fight you on this? You'll just come?"

"You've never told me that I needed to get my ass to Spokane before," Halley said. "Despite all the troubles we've had with Mom over the years. You've always just told me what was going on, and then left it up to me whether or not I'd show up."

"Oh," Caroline said. "I didn't realize that."

"So if you tell me that I need to come, I'll be there," Halley assured her sister.

"I've told you to come out here before," Caroline said after a few moments.

"Yes, after you've told me what was wrong. You've never just called and said that I needed to be there." Halley wondered how long she could string her sister along, without having to tell her about the nurse's call.

"All right. Then, yeah. I'll make sure you have a place to sleep tonight," Caroline offered.

"If it's that bad, I'll probably just spend the night in the hospital," Halley said.

Caroline snorted. "I suppose you're just going out to Spokane, see Mom, then drive back to Seattle?"

"I don't have any idea what I'm going to be doing," Halley snapped. "We can't make any decisions yet."

She didn't want to have to be in Spokane any longer than she absolutely had to be.

Especially if all she had to do was say goodbye to her mother.

CHAPTER 14

Halley hated hospitals. Not that she was in them that often. The posters with all the fake sympathy, the insistence that they were there to *care* for you, pissed her off every time.

Nobody cared. Not like that. Not that much.

She saw too much of the other side of things, of the side that the caring hid. Even Chet and Red, who *cared* for each other, had issues.

Hidden things. Dark secrets.

She'd left a message for both Phoenix and Billy, letting them know where she was. Chet and Red could just wait—she'd told Chet that she wouldn't be in touch with him for a week or so anyway. Amber Lee didn't have to know where she was either.

She'd actually been able to talk with Taylor as she'd started her drive east. At least Taylor's parents had had the grace to die recently, leaving her a nice inheritance and none of the shit dealing with aging relatives.

Taylor, of course, had been more worried about Halley than anyone else. She knew how difficult it was for Halley to go back to Spokane. As well as her awful relationship with her mother, and her true relationship with Billy.

Halley had promised to call or text Taylor whenever she had news, or even when she didn't, if she just wanted to talk.

It was good to have a friend like that.

The nurse let Halley in to see her mom right away, even though it was just after three AM by the time she arrived.

Her mom was in a shared room, on the side closest to the door, though there wasn't anyone in the other bed at this time. Halley didn't know if that was better or worse for her mother.

She recognized the woman lying in the bed that was partially raised, in the dim light. She'd actually seen her mother look worse than she did now, even with the tubes connected to her arms and the oxygen feed under her nose. They hadn't had to intubate her, so she could still talk.

Her mom's hair was dark brown, like Halley's. It wasn't as curly, though. Her face was round, like her sister's. Her apple cheeks and lips were red against her pale skin, giving her a fevered look. The skin on her neck sagged and had wrinkles, looking surprisingly old. The blue and white hospital gown peeped up above the white sheets. Mom probably hated it with a passion—not her colors at all. The arm connected to all the machines was outside of the blankets, bare and vulnerable.

Halley sat down on the chair next to the bed. Feeling strange, she reached out and squeezed her mother's hand. It was cool, but not cold. Was her mom running a fever?

She started when the hand in hers turned and squeezed back hard.

Sheila Brown stared with hard eyes at her daughter. "So I must be dying, for you to come back," she said in a raspy tone.

The voice shocked Halley. Her mother, for all her sins, had never smoked, and had a soft, melodic voice. Halley remembered when she'd been very young, listening for hours to her mother sing. That had been so many years ago, though.

Despite the coldness of her words, Sheila still held onto her daughter's hand tightly.

"You know that I couldn't let Caroline be the only martyr in the family," Halley said, joking. Tears were surprisingly close to her eyes. She sniffed, trying to hold them back.

"Wouldn't expect anything less that that sort of rivalry between you two," Mom said. She dropped Halley's hand and started coughing, wheezing loudly. "They won't let me put the bed all the way back. Seems I stop breathing when I lie flat on my back."

"You sound like hell," Halley said. While everything else looked the same, that voice no longer belonged to her mother.

"Thanks," Mom said. "The pneumonia's gotten worse. Can't get my oxygen rate back up." She raised her hand and wiggled her fingers. "These turned blue for a while. And the infection's spread everywhere. Can't seem to isolate that either."

"What, did it infect your blood?" Halley asked. She didn't think her mom had that type of pneumonia. She'd done as much research as she could online when her mom had first gotten sick.

"You'll have to check with them." Her mom started coughing again. It went on for longer.

At least she wasn't coughing up blood. But she wheezed horribly when she was finished, her breath whistling and her lungs creaking.

"Mom," Halley said. She stopped. Started again. "I have some questions."

Mom nodded. "Go on," she said. "It isn't like you to not just speak your mind. Or say whatever rageful, hateful thing you wanted to say."

Halley tried to swallow down some of her anger and at least sound somewhat polite.

"Who was my dad?" Halley said. She suddenly felt hollow, as if that question had taken up so much space inside of her that was now empty.

"Your what?" Mom said. Then she started cackling. "You know, I never expected you to ask about that," she said after a few moments. She reached out and found Halley's hand again. "You know, don't you?"

Halley nodded. "Found my half-brother living in Seattle," she admitted.

"Then what do you want me to tell you about?" Mom said, shoving Halley's hand away. "You weren't planned, that was for damned sure."

"So were you having an affair with Michael Evans?" Halley asked.

"You could call it that," Mom said. "Or you could call it blackmail."

"Blackmail?" Halley said, incredulous. "Against who? Or had he blackmailed you into sleeping with him?"

Mom started coughing again. Only this time, she started gasping as she finished. Her eyes grew wide as she fought for breath.

Halley realized that her mother could no longer get air in. She grabbed for the nurse call button and jabbed it hard, more than once.

The nurse came in almost immediately. She took one look at Halley's mom and said, "Could you please wait outside?"

Helpless, Halley left the room. She leaned against the wall as a second nurse rushed into the room, followed by a white-jacketed older female who she assumed was the doctor on call.

Of course, it would be just like her mother to die after

making such a provocative statement. That would possibly be the highlight of her life, quite frankly, making her daughter dance on her strings that way.

No. Her mother would survive this. Halley would ask her more questions.

In the meanwhile, there had to be something that claimed to be coffee someplace in this house of the dead and dying.

HALLEY FOUND her way to the waiting room at the end of the hallway. No one else was there. A muted TV was on the wall, showing an infomercial for some incredibly efficient vacuum. The colors on the walls were all soothing, she supposed, but really, they were just splashes of crimson and gold. The couches were overstuffed, and a reclining chair was in the corner.

Gratefully, Halley collapsed on the chair, stretching out and closing her eyes for a few minutes.

Her mom had been rushed out of her room and down to a different section of the hospital, where she was intubated. They were still trying to force air down into her collapsed lung. The doctor had talked about performing surgery later that morning, basically inserting a small tube into the lung and re-inflating it.

The problem was the infection. Her mom was running a high fever and she wasn't responding to the antibiotics. It wasn't a staph infection, so it wasn't one of those flesh eating infections that Halley had been dreading. The doctor wasn't sure what exactly she'd come into contact with. Just that her fever remained high. She'd tested negative for the most common strains of influenza.

They didn't want to take her into surgery when her

temperature was so high. But she wasn't responding to the chemical irritants they'd introduced to try to get her lung to re-inflate.

The surgical procedure was minimally invasive, and Halley had given the doctor the go-ahead to try it later that morning.

Halley closed her eyes in the waiting room. She'd been up all night. It was nearing five AM, now. Hopefully, no one would mind if she just rested here for a while. The nurse had offered to get her a chair for her mom's room, but there wasn't that much space. Besides, they were about to bring a second patient into the room. Halley needed some time to herself.

It was one of the ways that she'd always differed from all the rest of her family, her need for solitude. Being around other people all the time felt like sandpaper on her skin eventually, just abrasive and rough.

Halley fell into instant dreams where she was both being chased as well as chasing after someone. She couldn't ever see the figures on either side of her. She woke abruptly when she heard someone calling her name.

Blinking blearily, she realized that Caroline was standing there, next to her.

"Mom said you'd come in to see her," Caroline said. "Why aren't you in the room?"

"They were in the process of moving someone else in," Halley said as she pushed the chair back to a seated position. "Wait, how is Mom talking? I thought they had to reintubate her."

"They got her a white board and marker so that she could communicate," Caroline said. She sat down on the couch across from Halley.

Caroline looked round and plump, kind of like Amber Lee, though she was a blonde and not a redhead. She had cool blue eyes that regularly froze Halley out. Her smile was much more forced than Halley's—she'd never managed to fake a friendly, easy-going expression as well as Halley could. She looked tired, with dark circles marring her peaches-and-cream skin. (Maybe that was why Halley hated peaches so much.)

"Where are the boys?" Halley asked.

"Dropped them off with the sitter," Caroline said.

"Wait, what time is it?" Halley said, pulling out her phone. "Jeez. Eight ten. I didn't think I'd slept that long."

"So, what, three hours?" Caroline said.

"Yeah, at least," Halley replied. "I need coffee. Or the closest equivalent."

"The cafeteria downstairs isn't too bad," Caroline said. "They might even have pork sausage and eggs."

Halley couldn't help but smile at her sister. They did know each other a little.

"Should I look in on Mom first?" Halley said.

"Sure, but she's asleep again," Caroline said.

Halley stood and stretched, reaching first far over her head then bending over, touching the floor with her fingertips, then pushing and putting her palms fully on the floor in front of her boots.

"See, that's what having children does to you. Takes away all that flexibility," Caroline complained.

Halley bit her lip. She wasn't about to point out that she knew other women who'd had kids who were in as good a shape as she was, possibly even in better shape.

On the other hand, though, Caroline was right. Children did take away flexibility. If their positions had been reversed, with Mom in Seattle and Caroline out here, she wouldn't have been able to drop everything to come out.

They stopped by their mother's room, but she was passed out. The board was propped up beside her, in easy arm's reach. Her mother looked more compressed now against the white sheets, not quite bigger than life, as she usually did. Her skin was dull and almost gray colored.

What sort of blackmail had she been involved with?

Halley was going to have a chat with Billy about that tidbit soon.

She trailed after Caroline down to the café. It actually had an omelet station, so Halley was able to have eggs with all the fixings: garlic, spinach, greasy pork sausage and three types of cheese.

She might have to revise her opinion of hospitals if this was now the type of food they served.

Mind you, the coffee was still just water colored black. She was going to have to find some real coffee soon.

She sat across from Caroline in the eating area. It reminded her of the caféteria from college, with cheap wood and metal chairs, tables that were easily stackable, and a tough floor that wouldn't show dirt or scratches. Voices bounced off every hard surface, making it seem busier than it was, though only a few tables of the two dozen had occupants.

Caroline had picked up a sugar-free yogurt, part of her constant dieting. She looked wan in the gray light coming in from the windows, showing the overcast day outside. She was dressed in her regular office clothes, probably heading into work soon. It was a cheap looking blouse, off-white with a pattern of small violets on it, and a black pencil skirt. The front edges of her hair were pulled back out of her eyes with brown plastic hair clips. Caroline still looked attractive, if you didn't notice how little she smiled.

Then, she opened her mouth…

Halley shoved food in as quickly as she could, knowing the storm was brewing. She could see it in Caroline's eyes, the way she kept looking to the side and fidgeting, like a kid called before the principal.

Finally, Caroline turned to face Halley. "Mom said you were asking questions. About Dad."

Halley chewed as fast as she could, swallowing everything with the watered down coffee.

"No, she didn't," Halley said. "She wasn't that conscious. And I doubt she'd mention that sort of thing to you."

Caroline pressed her lips together in a thin line. Halley knew her sister was looking for the perfect insult. Finally, she settled on, "Fine. She didn't say anything about that. But you have been asking questions about Daddy, haven't you?"

"Why?" Halley said, tipping her head to the side. "Why should I be asking about Dad? What should I be asking about Dad?"

Caroline was three years older than Halley. She wouldn't really know anything about Mom's affair. She'd been too young at the time.

But she might have picked up on things going on between their parents when Halley had been too little to notice, say when Halley had been two or three and Caroline had been five or six.

"Daddy was a good man," Caroline insisted.

"He worked too hard," Halley replied, as she generally did. The father that she'd been raised with hadn't taken a gun and shot himself, but he'd killed himself nevertheless, working too many hours and not taking care of himself. He'd been a mechanic at a nearby shop and was always working weekends and overtime. He'd developed a cough one winter, and it just got worse and worse.

They didn't diagnose the small cell lung cancer until it was too far advanced. They gave him six weeks to live. He'd barely made it three.

If he'd gone to see a doctor instead of working all the

time, would the cancer have been caught sooner? Possibly. Though as it was small cell lung cancer, there was no guarantee that he would have survived it.

"He didn't work that hard his whole life, you know," Caroline said. "Only after you came."

Halley had heard that from Caroline before. More than once her sister had thrown into her face that everything had been perfect until she'd come along.

Had their lives actually been better? Was it the arrival of an unexpected baby? Or was there something else about Mr. Evans?

"You claimed that Mom had said I was asking about Dad," Halley said stubbornly. "What sorts of questions do you think I was asking? Or should I be asking?" She knew she was repeating herself. She didn't care.

"You should be asking about how long Mom is going to live," Caroline deflected. "You know that she already signed a DNR, right?"

"Yeah, you told me about it," Halley said. Mom had been saying for some time now that they weren't to take "heroic measures" to save her. Once her body decided she was done, she was going to be done. "Was kind of surprised that you got her back into the hospital."

"I couldn't just leave her in the house to die," Caroline said.

Halley didn't comment on how that would have left yet another mess for Caroline to clean up.

"What are we going to do when she's gone?" Caroline asked quietly.

"There won't be much of an inheritance," Halley insisted. "All her money's long since spent."

Caroline nodded. "I'm a co-signer on all her bank accounts. So there won't be any trouble there."

"She doesn't have a pension. All she has is social security, and that isn't much," Halley said. "Don't know if they'll pay out a death benefit or not."

"They will," Caroline said.

"You should keep it," Halley said. "Since you've been taking care of her for so long."

Caroline seemed nonplused at that. "Oh. Okay. Thank you. Is there anything of hers that you want?"

Halley shook her head slowly. "Nope. I took all my things and left years ago."

She pressed her lips together. She hadn't meant to be so bluntly truthful.

Caroline gave her a weary smile. "You know that Daddy left for a while after you were born, right?"

"No," Halley said, surprised. "That's the first I've ever heard of it."

Caroline nodded. "I barely remember it. I just remember Mom telling me that Daddy was taking a trip to Seattle. She'd originally said that he'd only be gone for a few days, but it felt like weeks and weeks before he came home. He'd missed my birthday. That's what I remember most."

Halley nodded. Caroline had always complained about her birthday happening just before school started, in September, that having to start school again was an awful present. Whereas Halley had been born in June, and frequently her present was getting out of school for the summer.

Had their shared father left for a while after she'd been born? Caroline was only three at the time. Or was that memory conflated with some other event?

"Do you ever remember some strange uncle or cousin coming around at that time?" Halley finally asked. "Just before or just after I was born?"

"No," Caroline said. "What are you saying?"

"Nothing," Halley said. She wasn't about to pursue this

line of questioning with her sister. Particularly not until long after Mom had passed. "Do you have a copy of Mom's will?"

Caroline shook her head. "No. But it's filed at Percy and Brown."

Halley nodded. She'd known that had been the case, and was glad that it still was. Though her mother had not always been sober, she did have an up-to-date will and had it filed with her lawyer. It was one of the few ways in which her mother stayed organized.

"Have you discovered any new caches of booze since she's been out of the house?" Halley asked.

Caroline rolled her eyes. "You know the one that's under the bathtub, right?"

"Yeah. And the fake shampoo bottle. Wasn't there also a false back to the medicine cabinet for a while?" Halley said.

"Yup. And there was a compartment under the sink as well." Caroline gave a shudder. "I swear, if there was ever a fire in that house, the place would go up in one great big ball given the amount of booze stashed away everywhere." She paused, growing sober again. "Do you think she'll be able to come home?"

"Of course," Halley said. "She's too stubborn not to."

After Caroline had left for work, Halley made her way back up to her mom's hospital room. The nurse had put a chair in the room, next to the bed.

Halley went in and watched her mom sleep for a while. She seemed more withdrawn than before. It was as if she'd always had something to prove, and now, wasn't sure what it was.

When the call from Phoenix came, Halley gratefully stepped outside the room to take it.

"There's been another murder."

CHAPTER 15

FUCKING VERN. Dalton couldn't fucking believe it.

It had been *his* idea to ride a cunt to death. Not Vern's. Dalton had been the one who'd come up with the plan.

They weren't bothering to hide the bodies. Fuck, let the police have their sloppy seconds.

Vern had had his car detailed so not a drop of blood remained in the back seat. Then he'd covered everything in plastic, so it would be easy to wash.

They'd all agreed that killing another bitch so soon would be bad. It would bring them too much attention, even if the cops didn't have a fucking clue who they were.

Still. Fucking Vern. He'd come out back behind the bar while Dalton was still riding the most recent one, waiting until Dalton climbed off. The alley was pretty grody. Dalton was probably going to have to trash these jeans, as the knees were covered in muck. The dumpsters stank back here, trash mixed in with the smell of urine from homeless guys taking a leak.

Dalton kept his back to Vern. Not that he was embarrassed or anything. They'd all watched each other before. He kept a lookout for someone stumbling up to the scene, one of the homeless returning or something.

From the way Vern was huffing, Dalton knew he was close.

Then the girl shrieked.

What the hell? You had to keep the bitches *quiet*.

Fucking Vern was stabbing her in the back while he rode her.

Stupid cunt. And Dalton wasn't talking about the bitch this time.

Vern finally caught a clue and stabbed his ride in the throat. Sheer luck directed the knife to the jugular and the bitch just collapsed.

It was nearly funny, seeing Vern there with his dick hanging out, wondering where the hell his ride had just gone.

"Damn it!" Dalton said. Rick was in the car already. He blocked one end of the alley with it, keeping the engine warm.

Dalton sprinted and slid into the front seat, with Vern right behind him, sliding into the back.

"What the hell?" Dalton asked, looking back at Vern.

Had he looked like that? With blood sprayed all over his face and hands? Vern looked like a wild man, with his straight hair sticking up everywhere, his eyes white and wide in his face.

Vern was drenched in blood, though. At least Dalton had had the sense to take off all his clothes and leave them at the scene. They'd all come from Goodwill, and he'd paid cash, nothing traceable.

"Dude!" Vern said, grinning, his teeth gleaming white against his blood-covered skin. "That was awesome!"

"Yeah, but she screamed," Rick said as he continued to drive sanely through the streets.

"You shouldn't have stabbed her," Dalton complained. "That wasn't cool, bro. That got her yelling. Should have just cut her throat."

"But it was so great!" Vern complained. "Man, riding her and stabbing her at the same time. My dick and my knife all working together. You've got to try it!"

"Not in the city we don't," Rick countered. "That was too close. People are going to find her much more quickly because she screamed."

Vern looked pissed. He turned his head and looked out the window before he turned back to Dalton with a smug smirk. "Now we're even. No, wait. I have a kill and a *half*. Which means I'm ahead."

"Fuck you," Dalton said, fuming and turning around in the seat so he could look out the front window.

Yeah, he was going to have to branch out on his own. That was too fucking close with Vern. Idiot didn't understand how to be *smooth*.

That was all right. Dalton had his own supply of Rohypnol. It was time for him to be on his own.

CHAPTER 16

Halley did *not* want to have to drive back to Seattle right away. She needed some rest. She agreed to spend the day in Spokane, as well as sleep there that night, then drive back to Seattle in the morning.

Of course, Caroline didn't understand that Halley had to get back to her job. Caroline didn't think Halley had a job. Just because she worked for herself didn't mean she could take time off without it causing issues.

Besides, there wasn't anything she could do here. Sit with Mom while she slept? What the fuck? Why should she do that?

The inactivity as much as anything else was making Halley crazy. She wasn't good at sitting in a single location for long periods of time. She'd only gotten through college by taking a lot of breaks. It meant studying for longer, but at least she'd gotten through it.

Now, sitting and waiting for Mom to die was pretty high on her list of things that were similar to hell.

The doctors still hadn't been able to perform the surgery to re-inflate her mom's lung. The fever had spiked again. They'd switched to a different sort of antibiotic, but as they hadn't isolated the cause of her fever, they weren't sure if it would help.

The next time Halley had touched her mom's hand, the skin was hot, as if she were burning up inside.

Mom woke up again around lunchtime. Halley had to grin at the instant irritation that crossed her mom's face when she realized she was intubated and couldn't just lash out or complain.

"Mom," Halley said. She reached out and touched her mom's hand again, squeezing it once before letting it go. "The doctors can't perform the operation to re-inflate your lung while your fever is still so high."

Mom nodded, indicating that she understood.

"They have to keep you intubated until they think you can breathe on your own," Halley added. "Can I get you anything?" Halley asked, trying to play the good daughter for once.

This tube out of my throat, her mother wrote.

Halley reached over and pressed the nurse's button. "We can ask," she said. "Don't know if it will do any good."

Mom nodded.

"So, about that blackmail," Halley said, trying for a casual tone.

Even intubated, Halley could see her mom's grin.

The words quickly filled the small whiteboard.

Sex for information and money.

Not how blackmail generally went. But Halley had no doubt where the power had been concentrated in their relationship.

Mom wiped the board as soon as Halley read it.

Before Halley could demand an explanation, the nurse came in.

"Mom wants to know if you can get the tube out,"

Halley said. "She promises to be good and to keep breathing," she added, nodding to her mom.

Mom also nodded, her eyes big and wide, like a little girl making a solemn promise not to go into the dark scary woods where her bestest friend lived.

The nurse said, "I can check with the doctor. But we're worried about your oxygen levels, only breathing with a single lung. The intubation also keeps your coughing down."

"Please check," Halley said. "Mom's going to go crazy not being able to talk."

The nurse pressed her lips together but nodded. "I'll send her a message. Is there anything else I can get for you?"

Mom shook her head. Both ends of her were connected, so she didn't have to get up to use the toilet. They were feeding her intravenously as well, one of the tubes connected to her arm.

"What kind of information?" Halley said as soon as the nurse left. Really, had her mom been some sort of spy?

Percy and Brown.

"The lawyers? Were you working for them as a secretary or something?" Halley said. She hadn't realized that her mom had once worked for those lawyers. She knew that her mom had always been friendly with the law firm, which honestly, now that she thought about it, didn't make any sense.

Mom nodded. She closed her eyes for a moment, pausing.

Halley could tell that her mom was exhausted just from this short interaction. Damn it! She really was sick.

"You go back to sleep," Halley assured her mom. "I'll be here later this afternoon when you wake up."

Mom didn't open her eyes again. She did nod, then her features relaxed, and Halley could tell that her mother had gone back to sleep.

Halley slipped out of the room, and then made her way

out of the hospital so she could walk for a while in the gray day, pondering what she'd just learned. She sent a text to Billy for him to call her as soon as he could.

Someone had set up a nice enough park between the hospital buildings. It was a small area, with a rock path all around the edges of it. No homeless, so that was a plus. The benches were all carved out of a pretty enough gray rock with curved edges, but cold as shit and still damp from the recent rain. The grass that sprang up between the buildings had been trimmed within an inch of its life. In the corner, flowers had been planted with a sign, "In memory of Gloria Finch," whoever the fuck that was. More flowers—probably left behind by a patient—were in a small vase attached to the side plaque.

Halley strolled around the small park once, studiously ignoring the nurse who was chatting happily on the phone on one side.

If Halley were near a gym, she'd go punch the shit out of a weighted bag or something. Damn it! She needed to do something. Anything.

Despite the wet grass, Halley left the artful rock path and strolled into the center of the area. There, she forced herself to close her eyes, bend her knees, and start to breathe in a deep controlled manner.

She opened her eyes when she started going through her Tai Chi form. When she couldn't go pound the shit out of someone, doing Tai Chi was the next best thing.

By the time she finished, Halley found that she finally had some level of calm returning. She checked her phone for any messages, then went in search of real coffee.

Luckily, just down the hill and across the street was a shop that at least had some promise, given the immense scowl the barista gave her when she walked in the door.

Maybe there should be a new scale for judging the

quality of coffee—two scowls for weak, five for perfect, ten for coffee that had to be sliced before serving.

Halley checked the Seattle news about the latest girl who'd been raped, then murdered. The MO was completely different, so the police were calling it a copycat. Of course, they weren't releasing the details. Had it been a different person in the gang of bad boys? Or was it really a sicko who'd decided to copy the first death?

The coffee Halley was drinking was slightly over-roasted for her taste, but it was so much better than the shit they served at the hospital. She assumed that was what kept this place alive—visitors from Seattle who knew good coffee.

Billy called just as Halley was finishing up her coffee. "What's up? What did you learn?" he asked.

Halley walked out of the coffee shop and back up the street. "Mom admitted to the affair. But not the details. She said something about blackmail."

"I wouldn't put it past my dad to blackmail someone," Billy said slowly.

"Don't think he was the one doing the blackmailing," Halley had to admit. "Mom said it was sex for money and information." She continued past the hospital and around the block. The neighborhoods here were sketchy, of course. Put a hospital in and the rents go down. But it didn't look that bad in the gray afternoon. Sure, maybe a few cars up on blocks. Nothing that looked like a drug den, though.

"Okay," Billy said slowly. "What sort of information?"

Halley nodded at the yuppie with his dog going the other way down the street before she continued.

"It seems that my mom, at one point, worked for one of the local law firms. Percy and Brown. Name ring any bells with you?"

"No," Billy said slowly. "Except that one of the firms

involved with a lawsuit against my father was named 'Little and Brown'."

"What was he being sued over?" She crossed the quiet street and headed back toward the hospital. Seemed the block dead-ended this way.

"I don't know. He was sued more than once. He always claimed it was disgruntled employees. If it hadn't been such an 'obvious' suicide, they would have had a list a mile long of suspects."

"Wow," Halley said. "Well, it's a new clue. Also, my sister claims that my dad went into Seattle for a while after I was born. Said he was supposed to only be gone for a few days but was gone for months. Don't know if he was also doing work for your family or if it's unrelated."

"I had no idea," Billy said. "There really won't be any records left. Did it happen just after you were born?"

"I don't know," Halley said. "Caroline was only three when I was born, turned four in the fall. Makes more sense to me if she was older, say, five or six, when something happened. Again, I don't know what went on, or if it's connected at all."

"I was certainly too young to remember anything," Billy said. "And my brother was younger than me."

"You could ask your mom," Halley said. She couldn't help but get that dig in.

"She wouldn't remember the name of mere help," Billy said truthfully.

Halley sighed, knowing that Billy spoke the truth. It didn't help sometimes that their backgrounds were so different.

"How is your mom?" Billy finally asked.

"She has a collapsed lung that they want to re-inflate using surgery," Halley said. "However, she's running such a high fever they can't. They're giving her more drugs to try to get the fever under control. In the meanwhile, she's intubated. We're communicating through her writing on a white board."

"Oh," Billy said. "How are you holding up?"

"I'll be fine," Halley said, though she knew that all of this was eating up what little peace and calm that she'd managed to find. "Did you hear about the next girl being killed?"

"Yeah," Billy said, his voice growing harsh. "It's not the same killer, though."

"Maybe it's the same group, and just a different person who did this last one," Halley said.

"They did both use knives, just in a completely different manner," Billy said slowly. "Plus, the second one screwed up. He stabbed her and she screamed. Though the people who heard the scream were slow to respond. It wasn't in the best neighborhood."

"It's the same gang," Halley said. "I'm sure of it." Even though there was no evidence.

"I can't tell you anything more," Billy said.

"I might have a sketch that you could use," Halley said slowly as she walked past the entrance to the hospital and back down the hill again. She explained about how she knew someone who had been approached, and while one of the guys had tried to get her drunk, another had tried to spike her drink. There had been a third one with them as well.

"Get me that sketch as soon as you can," he said. "We can use it to start asking people at the bar where it happened."

"Chances are, they won't go back there," Halley said. "I bet they've got a large rotation of bars to hit."

"They'll probably lay low for a week," Billy agreed.

"Though if there's more than one, they'll be egging each other on to do the next one," Halley said.

"Agreed," Billy said with a sigh. "Look I have to go," he said.

"And I need to see if they've agreed to take the tube out of my mom's throat. See if she can talk," Halley said.

"All right. Call me if you need anything," Billy said. "And let me know when you have that sketch."

"Should be tomorrow," Halley promised him. "Talk with you later."

Halley turned around and walked back up the hill to the hospital. It was getting late. Caroline would be stopping by soon. Maybe some of the other relatives as well, like the cousins who lived in town.

Mom was still out of it when Halley returned to the room. She sat quietly, waiting for the other shoe to drop.

CHAPTER 17

HALLEY WAS thankful that Caroline came in alone, without her two boys. The doctor vetoed taking out the intubation tube, so they couldn't really talk with Mom. Plus, she kept falling asleep. Writing was taking too much out of her. It didn't make much sense for them to stay any longer, so Halley followed Caroline back to her house.

The place hadn't changed since Christmas, the last time Halley had been there. The living room was overstuffed with furniture: a wide sofa propped in front of the TV on the other wall, a recliner that Halley knew was her mom's favorite, a coffee table in front of the sofa filled with toys and knickknacks, and a desk shoved in the far corner, covered in magazines and letters.

"May as well take Mom's room," Caroline said when Halley entered.

Nonplused, Halley nodded and hefted her backpack, walking through the living room with that awful beige shag rug and into the dark hallway with the three bedrooms and bathroom spread down it.

The boys' room was opposite Caroline's, at the end of the

hall. Mom's room was opposite the bathroom door. All of the doors were closed.

Halley paused, then pushed the door open.

There wasn't a lot there. A bed shoved into the corner opposite to the door, the covers pulled down showing a yellowed sheet and not successfully hiding the torn coverlet. White metal blinds covered in dust were shut tightly against the window. The closet door stood partially open in the other corner, inviting Halley to poke around in the rat's nest that was inside.

Mom's chest of drawers was there, a piece of furniture Halley remembered from her childhood home. It was painted white, but the wood had been artificially distressed and made to look like an antique. It was a piece of crap, really, like most of what they'd owned.

A TV took up a lot of the wall next to the door, along with another dresser. Halley remembered it as well, though the top of it had been taken down, the part that had held a mirror.

Halley didn't want to think too much about her mother living here, all the mirrors removed.

She changed the sheets, dislodging dust and grime as she did so. For a moment she paused, forcing herself to breathe, telling herself that the walls were not closing in on her.

Dinner was a riot with the boys. They were three years apart, five and eight, and rambunctious as only boys could be. Halley teased them and laughed with them, happy to listen to their antics.

She went to bed early instead of joining everyone around the TV set. She tried to work a little on her email, but honestly, it was just too much effort. She turned off the light and lay on the bed, noticing that despite the blinds, light still fell across the bed in solid bars.

Halley didn't know what time it was when the overhead

light was suddenly flicked on and she heard Caroline's voice calling to her.

"It's the hospital. Mom's gone."

MOM HAD EVIDENTLY awoken long enough to pull her own breathing tube out. Then she'd laid the bed all the way flat. Had she remembered that she couldn't breathe and done it on purpose? By the time the nurses got to her, it was too late. They couldn't resuscitate her due to the DNR. So she'd died on her own terms.

It was a sort of suicide, though Halley knew better than to bring that up to Caroline. She'd vehemently deny it. She wanted to blame the hospital, and had already brought up suing them, since Mom had contracted some sort of virus there.

Halley wouldn't agree to it, however. Mom had died. Halley had cried at first, but then the numbness had taken over.

Had her mom killed herself because she'd told Halley about her father?

Of course, it was easy for Halley to imagine some shadowy figure coming into the hospital and killing her mom once she'd spilled the news. The scenario was unlikely, given how stubborn her mom was.

Chances are, she'd decided she'd had enough, and just didn't want to live anymore.

Halley stayed in Spokane helping Caroline with the arrangements for the funeral. Everything was put on hold for a week. She replied to emails, rescheduled appointments, took some time with the boys.

She even helped her sister clear out her mom's bedroom, selling off all the furniture and giving the clothes away to a local women's charity. They found that the closet had a false back. Halley had been excited at first—maybe there would be hidden papers back there. But no, it only held more liquor bottles. Because of course it did.

The memorial was held a few days after Mom had died. Halley was surprised at the number of people who showed up. Since she'd retired, Mom had been going to bridge club and had actually joined a book club. Halley suspected that the book club was more of a drinking club, given the way some of the members were already tipsy that morning.

Everyone said nice things, of course. Halley found a gym that night where she could take out some of her anger at being stuck here in Spokane with a sister who was going to poison her. Unless Halley poisoned her first.

Finally, Halley was able to schedule her return trip to Seattle. The older boy was going to be moving into the bedroom Halley was staying in as soon as Halley left. Just the reading of the will remained.

Halley and Caroline went to the lawyer's office early that morning, so that Caroline only had to take half a day off from work.

Halley had never been to this law office before. It was in the historic part of downtown, in a converted building. The downstairs area was open and had its own food court. Halley found her mouth watering from the smell of the bacon and eggs being served, though she knew better than to expect any kind of decent coffee.

A wide staircase, made out of a bright wood with black iron fittings, rose up to the second floor. Halley was glad she wasn't afraid of heights, as it was out in the open. Despite the railing, it looked like it would be easy to fall off it.

Office doors lined the catwalk that went all the way around the second floor. A modern looking ceiling separated the third floor from the rest of the open area. The same bright wood and iron fixtures held up the catwalk.

The reception area of the office was decorated in leather and chrome, much more modern than Halley had expected. She could smell the expensive aftershave the lawyers used, a subtle clue to their richer clients that they were of the same class. The young blonde secretary appeared to be blockaded behind a huge wooden desk. A black-and-white photo hung behind her, showing Main Street in downtown Spokane as it had been a century ago.

The man who came out almost immediately to greet them was young, possibly just out of law school. Either that, or he had a serious baby face. He had round glasses, a sharp nose, and soft hands. His suit was black with white pinstripes and a little too large for him, making him look like an accountant who'd borrowed his big brother's clothing. He had thin lips and a forced smile, the kind that his pale gray eyes never reflected.

Halley would bet this was one of new attorneys, not anyone her mother had worked with. He led them to a conference room off to the side. It had that same mix of modern and old-fashioned that left Halley feeling on edge, with a broad black wooden table and modern chairs.

"We're sorry for your loss," he said as he sat down and pulled papers out of his file. After verifying Halley's and Caroline's drivers licenses, he started.

When he got to the part about the money and how it should be split evenly between the two girls, Halley and Caroline just looked at each other.

"Wait, can you repeat that?" Halley said.

The man read the number again.

"She had a million dollars stashed away that she never told us about?" Caroline asked, her tone uncomfortably close to a screech. "Did you know about this?" she said, turning to accuse Halley.

"I didn't have a clue," Halley assured her. "Is that amount right?"

The lawyer paused for a moment to consult a bank statement. "Yes, it is. Though there might be a little more, from interest," he added.

"Where did she get that money?" Caroline said, turning back to the lawyer.

"I'm sorry, I have no idea where her money came from," the man stated. "You didn't know about it?"

"Not at all," Halley said, shaking her head. Who would have thought that Mom had money stashed away?

But she did say that she'd traded sex for money and information…

"Where is the account kept?" Halley asked.

"Home Financial and Trust," the lawyer replied.

Halley and Caroline turned again to look at each other. None of the other accounts were at that bank. Halley didn't remember ever going there as a kid.

It was one of the oldest banks in town, though, that much she knew. And it was a bank that must have been in business thirty plus years ago, when her mother had been in a clandestine relationship with Michael Evans.

There weren't any other surprises in the will. Mom had sold their childhood home when she'd stopped working and had moved in with Caroline, three years ago. The sale had barely covered the second mortgage on the place. Their mother had given the extra to Caroline, to help cover the costs of yet another mouth at her table, despite the fact that Caroline now had access to free daycare, which had reduced her expenses significantly.

Halley walked out of the lawyer's office still in something

of a daze. She'd never even daydreamed about money coming in from Mom's death.

"What are you going to do with your half?" Caroline asked as they carefully walked down those too-open steps from the lawyer's office to the food court below.

"I have no idea," Halley said. She wasn't finished with her student loans yet. She could also completely pay off her condo. Though more money gave her the option of moving into a building that didn't regularly turn into a sauna…

"How about you?" Halley said. "Going to put it into some sort of trust fund for college for the boys?" They walked out of the building and onto the sidewalk. It was sunny and hot already, summer long since started in Eastern Washington. It was yet another thing that Halley liked about Seattle—more moderate climate, not as hot and dry. She didn't mind all the rain, either.

Caroline grimaced. "I don't know. I don't want to tell Dale about it, that's for damned sure."

Halley nodded. Caroline's ex was already a dick about paying child support. If he found out she'd inherited money, he was likely to be more of an asshole about it, not less.

"Do you want to buy the house you're in? Now that you have enough bedrooms for the boys?" Halley asked as they walked up the street, heading toward the public parking lot and their cars. "Might be nice not to have to pay rent anymore."

They'd parked next to each other, and stopped beside their respective cars. Caroline rested her butt against her black SUV. Halley took the same pose on her car.

They didn't look alike in the least. She kept coming back to that. But they'd been raised in the same household, and had shared a mother.

"Maybe we'll move to Seattle," Caroline said. "Get 'unstuck' as you've always urged us to do."

Halley felt her mouth fall open. "Are you kidding me? That would be great!" she said, trying to at least fake some enthusiasm.

She really didn't need her sister in her city, even if it meant she got to see her nephews more often.

Caroline just shrugged. "I could think of worse ways to spend all that money."

"Think of it as an investment, not as cash to blow," Halley suggested. She really didn't want her sister to go on a cruise or something, spending all that money and have nothing left to show for it.

"I'll do whatever the hell I want with that money," Caroline growled. "It's my share. You go and invest your own."

Halley bit her lips together so she wouldn't respond. She didn't want to provoke another fight, at least not at this time. Not when she was about to leave again.

"Will you come back next weekend?" Caroline finally asked.

"What? Why?" Halley said, startled. There was no reason for her to return. Mom's estate was done for the most part. They'd already cleared out her room. All that was left was the bank, and Halley was pretty sure she could start those conversations from home.

Caroline looked away, her arms tight across her chest, anger radiating in waves. Finally, she looked back. "You're supposed to be an investigator. Can't you come back and investigate where Mom got that money?"

Halley sighed. Caroline might be right about that. Slowly, she nodded. "I'll come back in a week or so, talk with the bank manager. See if we can go through the old statements, find out if Mom added to the account over time or if it was one big lump sum." She couldn't imagine her mother siphoning off much needed grocery money for this goose egg. Halley would bet that she'd received a large sum of cash from Michael Evans, and had decided, for some reason, never to spend it. Even after their father had died, and she no longer had to hide it.

Could Billy possibly track it on his end? See if he could find the payment?

"Good," Caroline said. "I'm going to hold you to that."

Halley nodded. "All right."

They stood there awkwardly for a few moments. Not friends. Barely sisters. Related through blood but not mind.

They didn't hug. Halley still made the effort, reached out and squeezed Caroline's bicep. "I'll see you later."

"Later, then," Caroline said, turning and getting into her car, driving off before Halley did.

Halley suspected that her sister had some contradictory feelings, just as Halley did, about their mother's death. It was both a relief as well as a sad thing.

But for now, Halley couldn't really think about that.

It was time to return to Seattle.

And to stop some killers.

CHAPTER 18

Halley took a long hot shower as soon as she reached her place. Not that being in Spokane had left her feeling dirty or anything. She'd just needed to wash off the drive, ground herself again in Seattle.

It was sunny and dry on her side of the mountains as well. Halley had spent time on the drive thinking about her future, making plans about what she was going to do with her inheritance. It would be taxed, she was certain. But even after taxes, it was going to be a hefty chunk of change.

She was absolutely going to pay off what remained of her school debt, though there wasn't much. Should she pay off her mortgage? Get a new place? She just didn't know.

Before she'd left Spokane, she'd left messages for both Phoenix and Billy that she'd be back in town later that afternoon. She called and chatted with Taylor for a bit on her drive, commiserating with Taylor's latest art project and how well it wasn't going.

Now that she was back home, Halley felt at loose ends. She couldn't go tail Red again, not until after he finished work for the day. She'd rescheduled her new client meetings for next week, as she hadn't been certain when she'd return from Spokane. She knew that she should nap despite the fact that she wasn't that tired. It took her a while to turn her brain off and get some much-needed rest, her bed a welcome oasis after sleeping on what had been her mother's bed for over a week.

Halley was disoriented when she first woke up, not remembering where she was. It took her a few moments to groggily reach for the ringing phone.

"So, are you ready for some undercover work?" came the cheery voice at the other end.

"Phoenix?" Halley said, rubbing her eyes.

"Yes, it's me, dear heart," they responded, their voice modulated back up into their dulcet tones. "We should meet for dinner."

"I need to wake up and drink a gallon of coffee," Halley grumbled. "Then, yeah, we can have dinner. But what did you have in mind when you said undercover work?"

"You'll see," Phoenix said. Halley could just see the smug smile on their face. "Meet me at Jackson's, down on Tenth, at seven."

"I'll see you then," Halley promised. She made herself get up, threw some clothes on, then caught a bus downtown to trail after Red for a while.

Red, however, merely went from his office straight to the house he shared with Chet in lower Queen Anne.

Halley turned around and went back through town, to meet with Phoenix.

Jackson's was a cute little bistro that proudly flaunted that tradition: it didn't blast music but let its patrons' conversations be heard; it had a lovely selection of baked breads and pretzels, along with some sausages; everything else was made fresh that day from what they'd found at the market.

The place was longer than it was wide, with a single row

of tables down the left, a long bar where patrons could also eat on the right. Seven PM was after the first rush, so tables were starting to empty out by the time Halley arrived.

The floor was done in large white tile squares with the occasional black tile accent. The tables were all marble with stylish chrome accents. Halley snagged a smaller one, seating herself on the red-vinyl and chrome chair.

A harried waiter came rushing up, looking askance at the empty seat until Halley assured him that she was waiting for a friend. After dumping off two waters in obviously hand-blown glasses tinted blue with bubbles rising up the glass, he hurried off, probably grateful that he didn't have to worry about her yet.

The menu was the same as always on one side of a photocopied sheet, listing their breads and sausages. The other side listed the fresh food for the day, along with a constantly rotating selection of wines that Halley never paid any attention to.

Scallops seemed to be in season, along with a monkfish fillet. Halley knew she shouldn't splurge out on a meal, but after eating her sister's cooking for a week, she also felt the need to cleanse her palate, as it were.

When the waiter stopped by asking if she'd like anything to drink, she ordered a homemade lemonade, hoping the man's head wouldn't explode.

People around her were finishing up their meals, dallying over coffee and dessert. Halley covertly glanced at their plates, trying to see what they'd had and had finished.

She guiltily started when a man suddenly appeared before her, placing his gloved hands on the back of the empty chair.

He looked a little familiar. His beard was neatly trimmed, along with his eyebrows. He cocked one at her as she tried to place him. He wore a black raincoat that fit him perfectly. Under that was a grey vest, black tie, white shirt.

Halley looked back at the hands perched on the empty chair. He was wearing black leather fingerless gloves, with a pattern of open holes cut through them, like racing stripes.

Finally, it all clicked. Halley shot her eyes back to the face. She swallowed, before she said, "Marc, I presume?"

"Exactly, dear heart," she heard.

It wasn't Phoenix's cultured voice. Instead, the tone was deeper, a little rougher.

Halley shook her head but gestured to the open chair and said, "Please, do join me."

Phoenix—Marc—beamed at her. "Thank you."

"Which pronouns would you prefer?" Halley said after taking a sip of her lemonade to clear her throat.

"I suppose I could be utterly ordinary and say he/him," Marc replied, much amused.

"It's up to you," Halley said. "I'll try to correctly use whatever you'd like."

Marc nodded. "I know. I appreciate it. So yes, for Marc, let's go with the male set. At least for now. Just one more thing to distinguish between the two."

"Any particular reason for, uhm, this transformation?" Halley had to ask.

"Aren't we going out hunting for a killer tonight?" Marc asked, seemingly perplexed.

"Not dressed like that, you aren't," Halley said bluntly. At Marc's shocked expression, she continued. "Don't get me wrong, you look fabulous. But you're also dressed like a natty gay man. The places we're going, the sorts of bars I'm going to need to start trolling—you're going to stand out. And that's bad. We need to blend in."

Marc sighed and thought for a moment. The harried waiter came up, took their orders, and rushed off again.

"Is he the only one here tonight?" Marc mused.

"Nope. I've seen two others," Halley assured him. "He's just that much of a rush junky, I believe."

"Ah. That explains it," Marc said. "So this won't do?" he inquired, gesturing at his outfit.

"I'm sorry dear heart, but no, it won't," Halley said. "However, can I just tell you thank you for showing me this? I know it wasn't easy for you."

Marc nodded. "You are one of three of my acquaintances who has become familiar with this expression of myself."

"Again, thank you," Halley said. "But if you insist on coming with me tonight, you're going to have to wait in the car."

"You need rough trade," Marc said with a smile. A little of Phoenix's dulcet tones came back in at the suggestion.

"Or frat boy," Halley said. "These bars are going to have a mix of both."

Marc thought for a moment before he replied. "I may have all the pieces, but I may also have to go shopping." He sighed as if that were going to be a huge chore to take on, when Halley knew that Marc lived for shopping for clothing.

Though that might only have been for Phoenix, and not this male person who shared space with them.

"I still want to start going to bars out in Sodo tonight," Halley said.

"No," Marc said bluntly. "Not alone."

"Nothing's going to happen to me," Halley assured him.

"And if you've been drugged? What will happen then?" Marc said.

"I won't really be drinking," Halley assured him. "There will be a wet patch under my chair where my drink will end up." She'd practiced that trick in front of the boys once, who'd both been in awe of their aunt who would only pretend to drink. It had been so worth Caroline yelling at all of them later for making such a mess.

"I will stay in the car, then," Marc said. He gave her a stern look. "I will not have you risking yourself in a stupid manner."

"Fine," Halley said, rolling her eyes. "It's good to see you," she added after a moment.

"I'm glad you have survived your trials and have returned to us," Marc said grandly, his tones creeping into Phoenix's realm again. "So tell me all about it. Your mother and the funeral and your sister and just everything. I want to hear it all."

Halley knew that he didn't, not really. Not unless she could make some sort of art out of the storytelling, or at least be catty about what her sister wore to the funeral.

It really was good to be home. And to know that her family of choice was there for her.

MARC DID as he said he would, and sat in the car while Halley went to a few bars out in Georgetown. She didn't have Bridget's sketch yet, so there wasn't anything to share with bartenders. She just wanted to get a feeling for the bars there.

She started with the distillery, though she doubted that the bad boys would go back there. They weren't likely to revisit the scenes of their crimes, at least not for a while, not until the pressure had eased off and the next big scandal or murder had taken the eyes of the cops off this area.

There was a bachelorette party going on in the distillery, a group of heavily drinking women being loud and obnoxious in the corner. Halley nearly turned right around and walked back out.

She still stayed for a short time, having a lemonade and not bothering with an expensive drink. The guys wouldn't be here. She kept looking at her watch as if she were waiting for someone. She also tried to get a feel for the group of women.

While more than one of the half dozen or so crowded around the little metal table were plastered off their asses, there was at least one person who was completely sober. Seemed they'd brought their own designated driver with them. That was good. It also meant that the women were less likely to be separated, as there was one sane head among them.

After reading a text from Billy that merely asked to meet her for lunch the next day, Halley stormed off as if she'd just been blown off.

Not that the barkeep was paying any attention to her. That was something else that she needed to keep track of—how attentive were the bartenders? In the places where the women were being slipped things in their drinks, she had to expect that they weren't at all.

Marc was reading something juicy on his phone when she walked back up to the car. She rapped on the passenger side window. He unlocked the car and let her in. She slid gratefully into the warm space. That bar had been freezing, and the temperature in the clear night wasn't much better.

"No luck?" Marc asked.

"Hen party," Halley told him. "Would have chased away any of the bad boys."

"I'm so sorry," Marc said.

Halley knew he meant it. Frequently, bachelorette parties showed up at the Double D or the other drag review locations. The women were often drunk and obnoxious, as if they had a point to prove about being "real" women or some sort of shit.

"I'm going to the serious dive bar next," Halley said. She slipped out of her nice enough jacket and slid on her gray hoodie, the one with the artful holes and patches up the sleeves.

"What?" Halley said with a grin at Marc's downturned expression.

"Here," he said, reaching over and musing her hair. He gave her a critical look. "You need brighter lipstick."

He reached into his bag and handed her a thin tube. Halley applied it, looking at herself in the mirror on the passenger side visor. Then she mussed her hair more, pulling the curls over to the side.

"Better?" she asked.

He nodded. "Now, go see if this next place is a viable hunting ground."

Halley nodded.

There were several men outside smoking as she walked by, nowhere near the required twenty-five foot didstance from the entrance. There was some awfully skanky pot as well. God, no wonder it was still called skunk weed.

The interior was brighter than Halley had expected. There were a couple of pool tables to the right, the bar to the left. The jukebox in the corner was rapping hard, something loud about the end of the world. A few people were gathered at the tables between the door and the bar. The group wearing leathers was all sprawled out, as if relaxing after a long motorcycle ride.

One of the bartenders looked up as soon as Halley entered. He was an older man, with long hair that went past his shoulders and probably should have been cut into a more modern style ages ago. He nodded at her as she walked forward, all ready to take her drink order. A second bartender was washing glasses at the far end of the bar.

"Just a lemonade," Halley said. "Waiting for a friend," she added.

"Coming right up," the man said, smiling at her.

As Halley handed the man a five-dollar bill, another man came up beside her.

"Hey, Bill," the bartender said. "What's shaking? Haven't seen you around in a week."

This wasn't going to be good hunting grounds for the bad boys, Halley could tell already. The bar staff knew their patrons. This was a neighborhood hangout, not a hunting ground.

It was good to be able to scratch another place off her list. Though she might add the name to a second list, one that she might revisit on a future night with Taylor in tow.

Halley went to two more bars that night. The first served food with alcohol, so a less likely place. People were there for late night snacks and munchies, not just drinks. Particularly given the cannabis shop next door.

The other place was similar to the distillery, except it served a lot of local beers. It catered to fratboys who were posers and who took their beer as seriously as Seahawks fans considered themselves the twelfth man. The bartender barely noticed her coming in, then ignored her.

That was part of the problem. Women were stereotyped as wine snobs, not vodka or beer snobs. So the sorts of places where the bad boys went, ones that were upscale like this one, would cater to a more male crowd.

Marc drove Halley home after the final bar she'd scouted, the pair of them agreeing to meet again in a couple of nights. Marc promised he could "butch it up" a bit, but Halley wasn't sure.

It might be much better for him to stay in the car and for her to go in alone.

Back in her condo, Halley took her Glock out of the gun safe and spent time cleaning it thoroughly. Though she'd cleaned it before she'd put it away, she cleaned it again, the familiar movements comforting.

It was a double stack, with a capacity of fifteen bullets, which while still legal in Washington wasn't everywhere. It was a larger gun with a longer grip that she found comfortable, but it was still slim enough to fit comfortably into the compartment in her backpack for when she wanted to carry it that way, or for the holster under her arm.

Halley wasn't going back out that night. Despite her nap, she was still tired from the events of the last week, with Mom dying and all that.

After Halley locked her gun away, she found herself sitting back at her desk again instead of going directly to bed. All the lights were out, and though the radiators knocked now and again, they were cool. She stared at the trees just outside her window, the occasional breeze tossing the branches up and down. The faint scent of coffee still lingered, along with the smell of the gun oil.

She was sad that her mom was dead. Angry that her mother had left such a mystery behind, had probably delighted in setting it up when she'd been alive. Halley would talk with Billy tomorrow to see if he could hunt down the transfer of money to her mom. It would have been thirty odd years ago, and chances were, Mr. Evans had hidden the transaction.

Plus, though it was a million dollars now, it probably hadn't been that much so long ago. Maybe it had only been a half million at the time. Should she reach out to one of the PIs she knew who did forensic accounting?

Still, it was a lot of money.

Everything felt unsettled. Phoenix becoming Marc. Michael Evans and her mom. Caroline and her. Even Victoria and Amber Lee.

Everything was in motion. Nothing was set.

Except her mom, burned and her ashes scattered at her request.

Halley hadn't kept any of the ashes, though the funeral home would have gladly provided her with a small, tasteful, expensive urn. What the fuck would she do with it? Take it to the gun range and shoot it?

Wearily, Halley made herself stand up and go to bed. Though the morning might not bring any answers, sitting there wasn't going to get to them either.

———

Halley sat in one of the shared office space desks, looking at the printout of Bridget's sketch, sipping her second—third —who was really counting—cup of coffee that morning.

The sketches didn't give Halley much to go on, unfortunately. She knew that Angel had done her best. But the features of the face were vague, just blank eyes and a pasty smile.

He looked like a frat boy, like the hundreds of frat boys she'd seen in bars recently.

The killers were blending in with their pack. Probably still raping women, but at least they hadn't killed another one. At least, not yet.

Her phone buzzed, showing Phoenix was on the line.

"Dear heart, how are you?" Phoenix gushed.

"Fine," Halley said, wary. "What's up?"

"I know I said that I could come as a more regular Joe," Phoenix said. They sighed. "I'm just—I'm not sure I'm up for the task."

"It's all right," Halley said immediately. "I still appreciate meeting Marc."

"I know. I just—I feel as though I'm letting you down," Phoenix said. "Not living up to my side of our partnership."

Halley rolled her eyes. "We don't have any formal agreement, you know. It'll be okay. I'll be fine."

"But you might not," Phoenix said. "Particularly since I know you, and I know that you're planning on going back out hunting tonight."

Halley sighed. Phoenix was right. Halley was going out that night, every night, hoping to find the killers before they snuffed out another life.

"So you need to text me the address of where you're going, every time, before you walk through the door. That way, if something happens, all you need to do is to send me 911," Phoenix said, sounding proud of themself.

"I could do that," Halley said. She hadn't been anxious about going out again on her own. However, having this sort of safety net made her feel better.

"And take your gun!" Phoenix said. "Promise me that too."

"I will," Halley said. She'd been thinking about that since the previous night. She was going to start carrying it with her. And she needed to get to the gun range—maybe later that day—to keep up her skills.

"Good," Phoenix said. "Thank you."

"Thank you for being my support," Halley said. She meant it.

"Kisses!" Phoenix said, hanging up.

Halley shook her head and went back to studying the printout. It wasn't enough to show any of the bartenders in the area. She still took the time to memorize the features, on the off chance that she ran into this bad boy.

What would she do? She played out the scenarios. Contacting Phoenix. Contacting Billy. Alerting the bartender, though she doubted that would do any good. Over and over again, so that the actions would become second nature.

She didn't allow herself to fantasize about taking the guy out back and shooting him, though that was tempting as well.

Finally, Halley felt as ready as she was going to be. May as well let the games begin.

TAYLOR WENT with her that night. They pretended to get into an argument at every bar, then would make up and be best friends again before they walked out. However, their act didn't draw anyone to them, no guys trying to get Halley drunk when she was on her own.

In addition to carrying the Glock, Halley had Victoria's phone tucked into her purse. She checked it in every bar they went to throughout the evening to see if it had connected to its old companion.

It felt good to have the Glock hidden under her jacket. However, the next night, when it was warmer, she switched over to a smaller purse that had a hidden compartment in the back, that the Glock just fit into.

Halley started to go out every night. It was grueling, going to loud bars and spending time out when she really wanted to be at home snug in her condo. Billy had tried yelling at her when he found out, but his heart hadn't been in it. He understood the need to solve the case, even at such a cost.

May passed, and June came, the weather shifting between too warm and too cold. She'd told Chet about Red's "second life." He'd cried when she'd let him know, tears of relief, he assured her. He also sent her a pair of tickets to the next Men's Seattle Chorus concert, later that summer.

The bank hadn't been able to tell Halley much. Seemed that Mom hadn't used that bank from the beginning, but had transferred almost the entire sum several years ago from a different bank to this one. She'd done it years ago, before the banking laws had gotten so strict about proving that you weren't a drug lord when you made a large deposit.

Billy also hadn't been able to find anything, hadn't been able to trace the money leaving his father's accounts. So another dead end.

It was the night before Halley's birthday, mid-June. She was alone in Sodo, in one of the seedier bars. Pinball machines were lined up on either side of the door, the constant electronic chatter making Halley want to shoot someone.

She'd been to this place before. It reminded her of the vodka bar in Georgetown in many ways. They didn't serve specialty liquor but they did have an impressive array of local beers. She always rolled her eyes at the names, like Starshower and Ghost Family, as well as the fancy tap handles used for each.

One of the reasons she'd returned to this place was because the bartenders would only serve her if she waved money at them, and sometimes not even then.

She was so tired of the bar scene. So tired of this chase. She couldn't just keep charging Amber Lee for her drinks, though the other woman swore she was fine with it.

"You by yourself?" Halley heard a young man's voice from beside her.

She turned her head to glance at her new companion. It had surprised her how infrequently she'd been hit on as she'd traversed from one bar to the next. Maybe she gave off "cop" vibes, as Phoenix had proclaimed more than once. Plus, almost all the drag queens she knew said she was a little too butch for their tastes.

It took Halley a few moments before she responded.

"Yeah," she said. She turned her face back to her drink, hiding her expression. "All alone. Mom died two weeks ago."

She was just a girl by herself, having herself a pity party.

The perfect victim.

Particularly for the guy next to her, who bore a striking resemblance to the artist's sketch she still carried in her purse, tucked in beside the compartment that held her Glock.

"That's awful," the guy said. "Here, I know just the thing to cheer you up."

He ordered her a Lemon Fizzy Drop, whatever the hell that was.

"I'm Dalton, by the way," he said as way of introduction. Didn't bother to shake her hand, though.

"Sheila," she said, taking her mom's name. Might as well. "You here alone too?" she asked innocently, taking a quick peek over her shoulder to look at the rest of the bar.

There, to her right. A table with two guys sitting at it. One light haired, the other dark. Might be his buddies.

Halley turned back to Dalton with a vacuous smile.

"Yup," Dalton assured her. He gave her a wink. "They were too boring to come out tonight."

"Need better friends, dude," Halley said.

"Don't I know it!" Dalton said, rolling his eyes. "You'd think they'd already have watched enough baseball by now, you know?"

Halley nodded. The bartender delivered a cocktail in a tall glass. Just from the smell of it, Halley knew that it was mostly alcohol, with maybe a teaspoon of lemon thrown in at the end.

"I don't drink very often," Halley admitted to Dalton as she took her first sip. "Wow. That's good though." It honestly was. The bartender had put in enough simple syrup to cover the medicinal alcohol taste, while the lemon was tart enough to balance it out.

Dalton gave her a big grin. "So here's to not being boring. To breaking out of the pack and going on our own."

"Here's to being alone," Halley said, remembering her cover story as she clinked glasses with him.

She pretended to take a big gulp, though much of it actually dribbled down the side of the glass.

"So tell me, not boring Dalton, what do you do when you're not out being not boring?" Halley said, trying to flirt.

"I run a call center, downtown," Dalton said. "You wouldn't believe how lazy some of the people are there. They just pretend to make calls, or listen to calls. You have to track them every second of every day."

Halley nodded, supposedly impressed. She would bet, though, that Dalton just worked at a call center and didn't manage one. He didn't have that level of control in his life. He was at the beck and call of others.

"What do you do?" Dalton asked.

At least he could fake interest well. Halley spun a tale of working as a secretary for a shipping company, shamelessly stealing details from Caroline's most recent job.

Dalton kept encouraging Halley to drink, ordering her a second one before she'd even finished the first. Then he switched the glasses around, pouring one into the other.

The way he kept touching her glass made Halley wonder if the gang was changing things up, if he would be the one to drug her instead of his buddy.

Then she glanced over her shoulder. The two who'd been behind her were no longer there.

Did she have the wrong guy? Was Dalton really just trying to hit on her?

Crap.

She had drunk more than she'd planned to already. This was not good. She wasn't feeling dizzy, not yet. The room wasn't spinning. She was still in control of her limbs.

"That stuff is going right through me," Halley lied. She stood up, pretending to be much more wobbly than she actually was. "I need to go use the little girl's room. Excuse me."

She picked up her purse and left. Only when she started walking did she realized that she'd drunk even more than she'd thought. She was a *lot* more drunk.

The bathroom was tiny, with just a toilet and a sink. No changing table here. Not the sort of place you'd bring a kid, anyway. Stickers and posters covered the walls, the ceiling, even the corners of the floor. There was no rhyme or reason to any of it. The colors clashed, the bright pinks bleeding against the sickly oranges. It stank of artificial air freshener, a sickly pine.

Halley fished her phone out of her purse and put in a 911 to Phoenix. Then she knelt down in front of the toilet, lifted the lid, and stuck two fingers down her throat. She didn't know if puking would help, but she figured it wouldn't hurt.

After she was finished and she'd rinsed her mouth out with water from the sink she thought to check the other phone in her purse. Victoria's phone.

Which had just paired with a fitness watch, somewhere in the nearby vicinity.

Halley jumped at the loud knock on the bathroom door, frantically stuffing the phone back into her purse.

"Hey, everything okay in there?"

She recognized Dalton's voice.

"I don't feel so good," Halley admitted. Shit, she hadn't meant to say that.

She'd been drugged and hadn't even realized it. She'd been thinking that they'd stick to the same MO. She should have known better. The room spun, the colors of all the posters wavering.

"Let me in. I can help," Dalton assured her.

Halley knew she shouldn't. She knew that chances were, he was the killer.

Had he gone off on his own? Without his buddies? Had that been why she hadn't been able to find them?

"Just a sec," Halley said. She barely recognized her own voice. She sounded weak and tired. She washed her mouth out again. Everything in the mirror was fuzzy. Then she put her bag firmly over her shoulder, sliding her hand into the gun compartment before she opened the door.

Dalton was right there, pushing his way into the bathroom, slamming and locking the door behind him.

Halley stumbled back, nearly falling on her ass.

"Aw, come on, I just want to help," Dalton tried to assure her.

He looked different under the brighter light of the bathroom. His eyes were fevered and he had red points on his cheeks.

"Let me out of here," Halley said. She tried to pull the gun out of the compartment but it was stuck.

"Shh, it's okay, I'll take care of you," Dalton said with a feral grin. He yanked her purse out of her hands and threw it beside the door.

Shit. Halley tried to focus her eyes. Her head was pounding. She'd been so stupid thinking she could do this on her own. She felt like throwing up again.

She took a deep breath. She was uncoordinated. But she still knew how to fight, how to defend herself.

All that time in the dojo needed to start paying dividends, right the fuck now.

Dalton tried to rush her. She struck the side of his head using the heel of her hand. She'd aimed for his temple, struck his cheek hard and whipped his head to the side instead.

"So you want to play rough?" Dalton asked, taking a step back and grinning at her.

Fuck. Halley couldn't judge anything, not how hard she could strike, not distance, not anything.

He came at her again.

Training took over. She grabbed his shoulders and kneed him in the groin, hard.

Dalton bent over like he was supposed to, and Halley drove an elbow hard into his back, sending him sprawling onto the ground.

She knew she wasn't coordinated enough to continue the fight. She was barely in control as it was. She fled for the door, her bag, and her gun.

The door was locked. She'd forgotten that. She still had her gun though. She finally managed to fish it out before he'd done more than rise up to his hands and knees.

He bared his teeth at her, growling like a wounded dog.

A loud knock on the door startled both of them. Halley refocused the gun on Dalton quickly.

"Halley darling, are you in there?" came Phoenix's warm tones.

Halley sagged in relief. "I am," she said. "I've been drugged. Dalton is in here with me."

"This chick is crazy!" Dalton cried out. "She pulled me in here. She has a gun on me!"

Halley shivered. He was going to claim that it was all her fault.

The only proof she had was the drugs still in her system.

"Just open the door, dear heart," Phoenix said. "Billy is on his way too."

Tears sprang up in Halley's eyes, the relief overwhelming.

"Don't move," she told Dalton.

He growled again, but then called out, "Be careful! She has a gun! She's going to kill me!"

Halley knew it would be within her rights to shoot him. She could claim that he'd come at her again, despite his obvious attempt to lay himself an alibi. But she was drugged. Didn't know exactly what she was doing.

Phoenix knocked on the door again. "Open the door, dear," they said. "I'm getting worried."

"Stay down," Halley ordered Dalton. She removed one hand from her gun, noticing the fine tremor, then reached behind her for the latch.

Finally, Halley managed to unlock the sliding bolt. She took a step to the side to allow Phoenix in.

"Oh thank god you're here!" Dalton said, starting to rise.

"Stay down," Phoenix growled.

Dalton blinked, getting a good look at who he was facing. "What kind of a freak are you?" he said.

"The kind of freak who would happily take you out and make the world a better place," Phoenix said in a low, mean tone that Halley had never heard before.

"Don't try it, punk," Halley added, though Dalton was just a blur in front of her. She had no idea if he was going to try to rush the door or not.

"You need to put the gun down, dear heart," Phoenix said.

Their voice was so gentle and mesmerizing. Halley felt herself start to lean toward it. "He drugged me," Halley said, the words starting to slur together.

"I know," Phoenix said. A cool, gloved hand slowly slid across her fevered ones.

Halley allowed herself to relax, to let that cool hand push the gun down, aiming the barrel at the floor.

"You're going to be fine," Phoenix told Halley again. "Come now, it's time to go."

Wait, when had Billy gotten there? Halley hung her head in shame. She didn't want him to see her like this. She slunk away out of the bathroom pressed against Phoenix, who put an arm over her shoulders like they were old friends. They even had Halley's purse in their hand.

A female paramedic was standing in the hallway and took charge of Halley, asking how she was, if she could describe what had happened.

Everything was too fuzzy now. It was like looking through a Vaseline-smeared lens. She was too hot, too. Halley gave answers as best she could, happy to leave the bar and stand outside in the cool night air. She vaguely recalled a needle in her arm, though she didn't remember being asked to give blood. Then the night gathered her up and she slept.

CHAPTER 20

I*T TOOK* four months for the cases to be settled. Fortunately, "bros before hos" didn't turn out to be the case between the bad boys. At first, Dalton tried to blame Halley for everything. That didn't go well, not with the Etizolam (etizzy, as it was known in the streets) found in Halley's system.

Particularly not with the tablets found when the police had had him empty his pockets.

That was then coupled with the fact that he was wearing Victoria's fitness watch. He'd killed the GPS function, but he hadn't done a factory reset on it. The fact that it was still paired with Victoria's phone convinced Dalton to turn on his buddies, originally claiming that they'd been the killers all along.

The police had found Dalton's collection of close to fifty fitness watches, and were still working with the original manufacturers to find all the women they'd been taken from. Vern's collection of hair had also been taken into custody. And Vern hadn't cleaned his knife as well as Dalton had. Forensics had found blood encrusted in the handle.

The bros all turned against each other at that point. Rick had talked the most, trying to bargain his sentence down as he hadn't killed anyone. They didn't have a prolonged trial, as none of them tried to enter a "not guilty" plea. Everything was worked out ahead of time, the deals eventually presented to the judge for sentencing.

Halley was relieved that she hadn't had to go and testify, though she'd been prepared to. The problem was that she didn't remember most of the evening. She vaguely remembered going to the bar, but had it been the first one that night? The third? She couldn't say. She was just glad that Phoenix had insisted on her setting up a safety net beforehand, or else her story would have been very different.

The black hole in Halley's memory bothered her. She poked at it like she would a missing tooth. She'd always prided herself on such a good memory. It was awful not remembering.

Her training had saved her. She started going to Krav Maga classes twice a week, just to make sure that she'd be better prepared next time.

Because chances were, there would be a next time. There were still too many bros who thought that women just existed for their pleasure.

Amber Lee called Halley the day after the last verdict was handed down, and they agreed to meet at the same coffee shop the next morning.

The artwork was different, collages of newspaper clippings and hand-drawn art. Halley particularly liked the man in the boat, trying to lasso the words floating above his head. The barista was almost nice to her, merely nodding his head instead of sneering at her, particularly when he heard her order of the exquisite Colombian blend that was on special.

The rest of the coffee shop was the same, with multitudes of digital nomads working on their computers at the tables, though there were a few people actually talking to one another and not just sitting beside each other staring at their phones.

Halley sat at the end of the bar again, forgetting until she saw Amber Lee that the stools were a little too high for her. But Amber Lee came bustling right up, saying, "Stay there while I get my drink."

Halley did as she was told. Amber Lee was still round and pudgy, her red hair still thinning. But she looked better than she had. She had a serenity about her that had been distinctly missing before. She was still in a badly matched blouse and pants—the yellow stripes in the shirt did not go with the green in her pants at all—as well as sensible, scuffed black shoes.

Carrying her hot chocolate and grinning from ear to ear, Amber Lee climbed up onto the chair beside Halley. "I can't thank you enough for the work you did," she said. "For tracking down and finding Victoria's killer."

"You're welcome," Halley said, uncomfortable. Amber Lee had thanked her many times before.

"I told the police to just destroy Victoria's phone. And the fitness watch," Amber Lee said, "when they're no longer needed for evidence."

Halley gave her a sad smile. "I'm glad we got them."

"I didn't do anything!" Amber Lee protested.

"You kept after me to find her killer," Halley said. "You paid for it."

"Victoria's insurance paid for it," Amber Lee said firmly. "I was just a conduit."

"Here's to catching bad guys," Halley proposed, raising up her mug.

"May you catch them every time," Amber Lee said, clinking mugs, then taking a large sip of her hot chocolate.

"So, what did you want to see me about?" Halley said

when Amber Lee didn't immediately start chatting away about something.

"I wanted to let you know that I've decided to move back to Texas," Amber Lee said. "I know, I know. The heat's awful. And men's attitudes toward women aren't much better. But I just can't face another cold, wet, winter without Victoria."

"I see," Halley said, though she didn't, not really. She understood not looking forward to the cold and wet winter, but she really hated the heat. Texas would be hell more months of the year than Seattle was.

"I'm not running away with my tail between my legs," Amber Lee stated firmly.

Halley knew that Amber Lee was no longer really talking to her, but to the voices in her head. Possibly to Victoria.

"I'm just a delicate flower and need that light," she continued.

"You need to be where you're most comfortable," Halley said firmly. "No one is going to think the worst of you for making yourself a true home."

"Thank you," Amber Lee said. "I knew you would understand. And what about you? Are you here for the duration?"

Halley smiled. "I am." She'd decided to go ahead and pay off her condo with the money her mom had left her. It felt good to be mortgage free. She might sell the place eventually, but for now, her roots were set.

"I'm glad I got to meet you, even if I am leaving now," Amber Lee said. "You and Phoenix."

Halley nodded, though she wasn't sure what the relationship had been between the pair of them. Phoenix claimed that they talked on the phone regularly with Amber Lee, though Halley had no evidence of that.

After Amber Lee had said goodbye, Halley put in her own call to Phoenix. She and Marc had gone out to dinner a few times during the last four months. She still didn't know what had happened to Marc, but she suspected it had been violent. Phoenix had joked more than once that the case had brought up bad dreams of poor makeup and wig selection.

Not that they would ever make those sorts of choices now.

They agreed to meet for dinner later on. Halley suspected she'd see Marc, but she never knew.

Humming, Halley finished her coffee and went back out to follow her most recent case, a lawyer who was absolutely fucking his secretary. Halley just wanted a few more photos of the pair of them kissing at lunch before she presented them to her client.

As Halley had suspected, Marc did show up for dinner that night. They were meeting at a new Italian restaurant on Pill Hill—the neighborhood just south of Capitol Hill, where all the hospitals were located. The restaurant was set up like an old Italian restaurant, the kind you'd see in movies: red-and-white checked tablecloths and candles in old wine bottles on every table; wait staff in white shirts, black ties, and black aprons; and scratchy opera playing.

Marc walked in a few minutes after Halley was seated. He wore his usual dapper suit, brown wool with flecks of green in it, as well as a sequined black tie. Black fingerless gloves covered his hands, of course, hiding the damage there.

Before Marc sat down he froze for a moment, cocking an ear and listening intently.

"Ah, Maria Callas," he said, identifying the opera singer. "Amazing voice."

Halley wondered if she would have gotten the same

response out of Phoenix, or if they would have declared the noise as god awful and insisted that they change venues.

"So how are you?" Marc asked as he perused the menu. "Now that the trials are all over?"

"Better," Halley said. "I still wish I could remember what happened." Phoenix had told her all the details that they knew, but Halley still found the hole in her memory bothersome.

"You need to let it go," Marc intoned. "Move on."

Halley suspected he was quoting from his own story, the one he told himself about his own trauma.

"I know," Halley said. "And it will be easier now that the trials are all finished. I'm glad they all went to prison." Dalton and Vern were both given fifty years, while Rick had the lightest sentence of all of them—merely a dozen years due to the plea bargains.

Halley knew that didn't mean much. They'd be out in twenty to twenty-five for good behavior. If they survived prison. Inmates didn't think much of rapists.

"And Amber Lee is leaving town," Halley added.

"Yes," Marc said. "Phoenix talked with the poor dear this morning. Seems she just wants some warmth again."

Halley nodded. They ordered, then talked lightly of other things, the show that Phoenix was directing, the latest case that Halley had, the review of the new restaurant that they were going to have to try next month.

It wasn't until after dinner, when they were sharing a zabaglione while Halley sipped her most excellent espresso that the conversation turn serious.

"I was attacked, you know," Marc said, sitting back in his chair, waving a spoon indicating that Halley could have the last of the creamy deliciousness of their dessert.

Halley didn't say anything, just listened quietly.

"There were ten of them," Marc said.

"Jesus," Halley breathed out. It had been bad enough just with Dalton and the nightmares he'd inspired. She worried that she'd actually been raped and didn't remember, though she knew that wasn't the truth.

"I used to accompany myself on the piano," Marc said. "I don't have the reach, now. Or the strength."

Halley nodded. She'd seen fine tremors in Phoenix's hands more than once.

"But I moved on," Marc said, his voice growing stronger. "As Phoenix."

"I'm glad you did," Halley said, giving him a smile.

"It's been good to make a few appearances as Marc again," he said. "But he might go back into the closet, as it were. Now that this case is over."

"Okay," Halley said. "I want you to be happy."

"Thank you, dear heart," Marc replied, using Phoenix's dulcet tones. "I have been happy with you."

Halley felt her heart start pounding. Was Phoenix breaking up with her? Crap! While they weren't partners, not really, they had become friends.

"But I think I react better as Phoenix in these situations," Marc continued.

"So you're not breaking up with me?" Halley teased.

"Well, maybe Marc is, darling," he replied with a sly smile. "But never fear. Phoenix still has your back. We will both continue to rise from the ashes and dazzle all the unbelievers."

"Cheers to that," Halley said, raising her coffee cup.

Because what would a girl do without her genderbending sidekick?

CHAPTER 21

Billy called the next day, wanting to get together for happy hour tomorrow afternoon. Halley was happy to meet with her half-brother, though they hadn't had many new clues about their parents' respective pasts.

He was in a warm navy blue suit that fit him well, with a light blue shirt and a red power tie, of course. He looked tired—the precinct had just had an "all hands on deck" situation with a triple murder in Belltown the week before. He carried the brown leather messenger bag that he used as a briefcase.

They met at a wine bar that was just off Fifteenth, and ordered the cheese and meat plate to split between the pair of them. It was quiet in the bar. The corner they found was cozy. Halley knew that the bartender probably had thought they were a couple, given the sly smile he gave her.

Halley wasn't in the market for finding another boyfriend. Or a girlfriend, though she'd never actually swung that way. Still didn't find women all that attractive, though Phoenix would say she just hadn't found the right one.

Billy talked in broad outlines of the current cases he was

working on. Halley did the same. Finally, Billy pulled out a photograph from his bag and slid it over to Halley.

"Do you recognize anyone there?" he said casually.

The photo was a bit grainy, and the lights in the bar were dim. Still, it only took her a few moments to recognize the man standing behind their shared bio-dad.

It was her own father.

"This was taken when I was three," Billy commented. "I went checking through the old pictures once you told me about Caroline's recollection that your dad went missing for a few months."

Halley stared at the picture. It was absolutely the man she'd always thought of as her father, standing shoulder to shoulder with a few other men she didn't recognize. He was wearing a suit, which was odd. She didn't remember him ever wearing a suit. He had a smile on his face but the expression looked strained.

"Who are these other men?" Halley asked.

"They were investors in my father's company," Billy replied. "That one, standing beside your dad with his hand on his shoulder, is my Uncle Larry."

"Alive still?" Halley said.

"Yes," Billy said with a sly smile. "Want to go meet him? Say, at seven this evening, for dinner?"

"Of course," Halley said. Finally, they were going to get somewhere!

"I don't know how much he knows about our father's murder," Billy warned. "However, he might be able to tell us something about this picture."

"Awesome," Halley said. "So, am I your sister? Your girlfriend? Just a concerned citizen?"

Billy's expression grew thoughtful. "Just a friend who saw this photo and is interested in what her father is doing there," he said eventually.

They gamed through a few scenarios, taking different parts and roles, before they finally headed out of the city, over to Belleview, to meet Billy's uncle at a fancy steak house.

———

HALLEY KNEW that the steak house was trying to give their diners the impression that it was very rich, with all the leather and heavy wooden furniture, but it just felt old and stuffy to her. The floors were all done in a thick carpet that was probably hell to clean. She was just as glad that the light were low so she couldn't see the dirt.

Uncle Larry turned out to be tall, like Billy and Halley. He was a fit man, tanned, with a lion's mane of white hair. He wasn't wearing a suit, just a leather jacket that would have looked better on a man much younger, plain lime-green shirt and jeans.

"Didn't expect you to bring a date, young man," Uncle Larry said as he walked up to shake Billy's hand.

"She'd just a friend," Billy assured him.

"Really?" Uncle Larry said, turning and giving Halley a teasing grin.

"Really," Halley assured him. He had a solid grip and shook her hand firmly. "Mr. Evans?" she hazarded.

"No, call me Uncle Larry, like this young man will inevitably do," he said.

The waitress took their order shortly and Uncle Larry started with stories meant to embarrass Billy in front of his new friend, though neither of them were embarrassed.

Billy didn't bring out the picture until after Halley had gorged herself on a wonderful ribeye and was slowly sipping her after-dinner coffee.

"Can you identify the men in this picture?" Billy asked as he slid the photograph across the table.

Uncle Larry looked at it, then looked up at Halley.

"Halley Brown, you said, right?" Uncle Larry said, a canny look shutting down his formerly open expression.

"Yes," Halley said.

"Any relationship to Emmet Brown?" Uncle Larry said, pointing directly to her father.

"He was my dad," Halley said, raising her chin lightly, feeling defiant.

Uncle Larry nodded. "I thought you looked familiar. Your father was a good man. Hard worker. Spent the summer working as a manager for Billy's dad in the Brighton factory."

"Really?" Halley said, surprised. Why would her father do that? He was a mechanic, had been one all his life as far as she knew.

"It was just for one summer," Uncle Larry said, nodding. "When I asked Michael where he'd found such a gold mine, he said he'd had to cast his net wide. Said it cost him a pretty penny, too."

Halley wondered suddenly if some of the money from the inheritance had come from that summer as well, and not just from Mr. Evans and the blackmail.

She turned to look at Billy, who just shrugged.

Billy had a pensive look on his face. "The Brighton site. Wasn't that the place where the workers tried to unionize?"

Uncle Larry waved his hand dismissively. "Some people think they should get paid even for not working."

Halley didn't reply. Her dad had been a unionizer. She remembered that her dad had made sure the shop workers got more protections, were able to take time off when their kids were sick, got paid their required overtime.

Why would he be working in an anti-union place?

Unless his work there had convinced him he needed to organize people at home…

"I know, I know," Uncle Larry said, shaking his head.

"Those aren't popular beliefs. Back in my day, we did an honest day's work for an honest day's wage."

Halley pressed her lips together so she wouldn't respond that Uncle Larry wouldn't understand what either an honest day's work or a living wage was.

"I suppose that was why you invited me out to dinner, isn't it, young man?" Uncle Larry said, turning to face Billy. "Because you found this old photograph and your new girlfriend here recognized her father?"

"I'm not his girlfriend," Halley ground out. "Where were you the night that Michael Evans shot himself?"

"I was out of town," Uncle Larry replied. He seemed flustered. "Why would you bring up ancient history like that?"

"I was just curious, that's all," Halley said. She pasted that easy-going smile on her face.

Uncle Larry appeared to buy it. They said their good-byes soon afterward.

Billy didn't say anything more until they got out to the car.

"He was lying, you know," Billy said. "According to statements given at the time, he wasn't out of town. He was at his club."

"Oh," Halley said. She suddenly felt much smaller.

"And you know that lawsuit that I said Dad was fighting? The one from Little and Brown? That was from the Brighton factory. It claimed that he was anti-union. Lawsuit was settled out of court."

"And my dad was hired three years later to break up the unions again," Halley hazarded. That would make sense to her, that her father wouldn't actually do anything to better his situation until he'd had it shoved in his face. His work at the Brighton site had made him into a firm believer in unions.

"Your dad wasn't that successful, I'm afraid," Billy said. "The employees voted to unionize at the start of the year. Factory was shut down not long after that."

"So do you think it was one of those unionizers who killed Michael Evans?" Halley asked.

Billy shook his head. "No, that was pretty far in the past."

"So we're back to square one," Halley said.

"No, not quite," Billy said. "You remember how Mr. Lewis and Kenny both claimed to be in the room when Dad shot himself?"

Halley nodded.

"I bet Uncle Larry was in the room too," Billy stated.

Halley sighed and they drove in silence, curving off the freeway and onto the long I-90 bridge that connected Seattle and its eastern suburbs.

The waters looked dark and stormy outside the window. Flashes of light filled the car as they passed under the streetlights. The city of Seattle stood like a beacon before them.

Halley still didn't know who had killed her bio-dad.

They were one step closer, though.

It was time to start questioning the family. Not her family, not the pitiful remains of that, Caroline stuck in her own dark hole in Spokane. Not her family of choice either, Phoenix and Taylor and her other friends.

No, the family of her other genes.

She knew Billy didn't want to do it. But someone was going to have to go ask Mrs. Evans exactly what had happened all those years ago.

It always came back to family.

Long may they reign in hell.

Leah Cutter writes page-turning fiction in exotic locations, such as a magical New Orleans, the ancient Orient, Hungary, the Oregon coast, rural Kentucky, Seattle, Minneapolis, and many others.

She writes literary, fantasy, mystery, science fiction, and horror fiction. Her short fiction has been published in magazines like *Alfred Hitchcock's Mystery Magazine* and *Talebones*, anthologies like Fiction River, and on the web. Her long fiction has been published both by New York publishers as well as small presses.

Find Leah's books on Knotted Road Press at (www.KnottedRoadPress.com)

Follow her blog at www.LeahCutter.com.

Reviews

It's true. Reviews help me sell more books. If you've enjoyed this story, please consider leaving a review of it on your favorite site.

Come someplace new…

Are you a traveler? Do you enjoy exploring strange new worlds, new cultures, new people?

Journey into the various lands envisioned by Leah Cutter.

Sign up for my newsletter and I'll start you on your travels with a free copy of my book, *The Island Sampler*.

I will never spam you or use your email for nefarious purposes. You can also unsubscribe at any time.

http://www.LeahCutter.com/newsletter/

Knotted Road Press fiction specializes in dynamic writing set in mysterious, exotic locations.

Knotted Road Press non-fiction publishes autobiographies, business books, cookbooks, and how-to books with unique voices.

Knotted Road Press creates DRM-free ebooks as well as high-quality print books for readers around the world.

With authors in a variety of genres including literary, poetry, mystery, fantasy, and science fiction, Knotted Road Press has something for everyone.

Knotted Road Press
www.KnottedRoadPress.com